her right against him. Take up where they'd
left off.

"Where would you like it, ma'am?" Jeeves
appeared next to them with a silver tray
filled with teacups and scones and clotted
cream and jams.

Seline closed her eyes. "Remind me to talk
to you about your awful sense of timing,
Jeeves."

The butler grinned at her, as if he believed
his timing was perfect, as he put the tray
down on the table near the long sofa. "Yes,
ma'am."

Just like that they were alone again.

And Ryder became doubly aware of how
very close she was.

And did something he definitely hadn't
planned to do. At least not consciously.

He kissed her.

Dear Reader,

"Well-behaved women rarely make history." This Laurel Thatcher Ulrich quote is one of many that grace our office walls. Women who push the boundaries of accepted behaviour are a popular theme for us, so when it was proposed that, along with Leslie Kelly and Julie Elizabeth Leto, we consider adding members to THE BAD GIRLS CLUB, we immediately signed on.

In *Taken*, Seline Sanborn is a sexy con artist. And self-made millionaire playboy Ryder Blackwell is the handsome mark. When Seline breaches his company's inner circle by posing as a successful account executive, Ryder falls for her hard. A one-night stand quickly turns into full obsession. But what happens when he wakes up to find the angel in his bed gone…along with an interesting chunk of his company's capital? Is he capable of redefining everything he believes about life and love and the law in order to be the one man skilled enough to earn Seline's trust and steal something worth far more than money – her heart?

We hope you enjoy every twist and turn in Seline and Ryder's unconventional journey towards happily-ever-after. We'd love to hear what you think. Contact us at PO Box 12271, Toledo, OH 43612, USA (we'll respond with a signed bookplate, newsletter and bookmark), or visit us on the web at www.toricarrington.net.

Here's wishing you love, romance and *hot* reading.

Lori & Tony Karayianni
aka *Tori Carrington*

TAKEN

BY
TORI CARRINGTON

MILLS & BOON
Pure reading pleasure

First published in Great Britain 2008
by Harlequin Mills & Boon Limited,
Eton House, 18-24 Paradise Road, Richmond, Surrey TW9 1SR

© Lori and Tony Karayianni 2007

ISBN: 978 0 263 86222 5

14-0908

Harlequin Mills & Boon policy is to use papers that are
natural, renewable and recyclable products and made from
wood grown in sustainable forests. The logging and
manufacturing processes conform to the legal environmental
regulations of the country of origin.

Printed and bound in Spain
by Litografía Rosés S.A., Barcelona

TORI CARRINGTON

Romantic Times BOOKreviews Career Achievement Award-winning husband-and-wife duo Lori and Tony Karayianni are the power behind the pen name Tori Carrington. Their over thirty-five novels include titles for Mills & Boon® Blaze® and Special Edition lines. They call Toledo, Ohio, home base, but travel to Tony's home town of Athens, Greece, whenever they can. For more information on the couple, their books and where they plan to appear next with a fresh batch of Tony's Famous Baklava in hand, visit www.toricarrington.net.

We dedicate this book to fellow lifetime Bad Girls Club members Leslie Kelly, Julie Leto and our shared editor Brenda Chin. And to bad girls everywhere: keep knocking down those walls and breaking through those glass ceilings.

1

IT WAS a temptation she couldn't resist.

Heat slid over her skin, igniting every nerve ending, making her hyper-aware of each breath she drew in. Tension. Anticipation. Longing. All combined in her muscles, clamored for release. Demanded she unleash the more primal part of herself kept under wraps for far too long.

It was July, it was hot and Seline Sanborn sat alone in her leased glossy-black Audi TT roadster convertible with the top down, her Dior shades parked on her nose, tendrils of blond hair stuck to her chin and lips. Yearning, pure and strong, shuddered through her. How long it had been since she'd allowed herself the indulgence of taking off her mask? One month? No, it was closer to two. Two months since she'd taken on the identity of conservative Carol Lambert, senior account executive moved to New York City from Seattle, Washington. Eight weeks in which she'd gained the confidence of the higher-ups at Blackwell & Blackwell Industries. Sixty days since she'd traded a lifestyle with few boundaries for long twelve-hour days, and nights spent reviewing carefully laid out plans rather than enjoying romantic sunsets with a special someone.

Then again, it had been time immeasurable since she'd spent a romantic anything with anyone.

Which probably explained why she'd decided to take the sporty rental car to her uptown lunch meeting rather than a taxi. And why she'd let the top—and her hair—down afterward.

Of course, the success of the meeting had also contributed to her desire to cut loose. If all corporate endeavors could be as powerfully engaging, she'd seriously consider hanging up her hat and going legit. The problem was that there was much more paperwork and tedium involved in the life of a corporate exec than big-ticket deals like the one she'd just brokered on behalf of Blackwell & Blackwell.

Or rather, just brokered on behalf of herself using a shell company she'd anonymously staffed through a temporary employment agency. A company that would cease to exist by this time tomorrow, guaranteeing her rush would survive at least as long…and the security the funds from she'd make off with even longer.

Which was why she much preferred the title of con artist. Forget that the job was the only one she knew. What other position would give her quick access to the type of money she needed? Not even Carol Lambert's nice salary could cover an overhead that went beyond the expensive leased cars and designer duds she needed for her cons. Well beyond.

Of course, the impulsiveness of her current actions went against one of her top rules, developed out of necessity: do not, under any circumstances, let your guard down until the con is over. And seeing as only a day and a half—thirty-six short hours—remained in her current job…well, her uncharacteristic recklessness was spotlighted all the more.

"It's a car ride, that's all," she said quietly. "What harm can come out of a car ride?" She pressed the power button for the high-end CD player. The guitar riffs of "Radar Love" by Golden Earring instantly drowned out the cautionary voice that whispered in her ear, along with the sound of the purring engine now idling at a stoplight.

Until the rumble of another equally impressive engine turned her attention to her left.

She smiled with deliberate pleasure.

It didn't take a car lover to appreciate the sleek lines of the XK Jaguar. But seeing as she knew the 12-cylinder engine that growled beneath the attractive hood inside and out, her interest quotient notched upward.

Too bad all she could make out through the heavily tinted windows was her own reflection. Which looked damned good, if you asked her.

She tilted her head and made a play at nudging her sunglasses halfway down her nose to get a better look at the driver even though she couldn't see him.

The response was a revving of the potent engine.

Seline righted her glasses and looked forward.

Having been raised in New York, despite the fact that she could no longer live there unless she was on the job, she knew times were few and far between when traffic opened in front of you. And this appeared to be one of those rare occasions when the big city and her many denizens offered up a precious gift of space and opportunity. She had every intention of greedily taking advantage of both.

She put the car into first gear, easing up on the clutch even as she floored the gas pedal. The car's back end immediately jerked as the back tires spun against hot asphalt. The Jag's engine revved louder in answer.

She watched the opposing traffic light. A moment after it turned red, and a split second before hers turned green, Seline released the brake and the Audi shot forward in a cloud of white smoke and burning rubber. She was no fool. She knew the Jag could do cartwheels around her car…if the driver was equal to her and if she played fair.

But she wasn't known for fair. For survival's sake, she'd learned to take full advantage of any opportunity to get ahead. In this case, literally.

She switched gears into third, then quickly into fourth, watching as the speedometer needle leapt upward.

The Jag easily caught up, staying even with her. Ahead, a taxi seemed to be at a dead stop in the middle of the road. She veered right even as the Jag swerved left, within moments the two of them running side by side again.

Seline shivered at the feel of her hair whipping around her face, the sound of the engine and electric guitar filling her ears, and the sights and smells of midtown Manhattan around her.

Damn, but this felt good. And it had been a long time since she'd felt good. Much longer than two months.

She and the Jag ran like that for another four blocks before the other driver blew his horn. She shot him a look, having noticed two lights back the white-and-blue NYPD cruiser parked at the next intersection. What she didn't know was if the other driver would have the guts to continue the street race or if he would drop back.

To her surprise, he kept up with her, even upping the ante as he blew past her.

The stopped squad car immediately turned right and gave chase after the Jag.

Seline thrust the gear into Neutral and made a squealing right-hand turn, then another, until neither the Jaguar nor the cops were any longer visible.

Yes.

Seline relished the rush even as she turned the music down, slowed to the speed limit, then headed back to the offices of Blackwell & Blackwell where she would have to play Little Miss Manners for the next four hours before knocking off work…with nothing but a saucy little smile to remind her of her brief excursion.

"THANK YOU, officer."

Ryder Blackwell accepted the speeding ticket from the unsmiling NYPD officer then leaned back in his dormant Jaguar and watched the patrol car drive away.

He'd purposely raced by the hot babe in the Audi, hoping to place her squarely in the patrol's crosshairs rather than him.

Then she'd turned off and rather than following her, the police officer had targeted him instead.

He grinned and shook his head, thinking of the provocative blonde in the black car—the personification of every teenage boy's dream. And, apparently, a grown man's, as well.

"Can I take that for you, Mr. Blackwell?"

He'd only been a block up from the Blackwell & Blackwell building when he'd been pulled over, so the red-haired, freckled-face valet who usually parked his car had sprinted over to meet him.

Ryder got out of the XK and tossed him his keys. "Sure, O'Malley. But why don't you take her through the car wash before parking her back in the garage."

"Yes, sir, Mr. Blackwell."

Ryder chuckled quietly as he retrieved his briefcase from the back of the Jag. He knew the nineteen-year-old valet would take the car for a spin first. But that's what hot July days were meant for. If you couldn't have a little fun in a kick-ass car on a day like this, what was the point? He would have loved the opportunity when he was O'Malley's age.

He straightened his tie and was crossing the parking-garage driveway when he was nearly hit by the woman he'd never expected to see again. Ryder squinted at her. At least he thought it was her. Gone were the trendy sunglasses. Up were the Audi's top and her wild blond hair. And if he didn't know better, he'd think she'd exchanged scarlet lipstick for neutral beige.

"I'm sorry, Mr. Blackwell," she said, looking everything like yet nothing like the woman who'd tempted him into a ticket. "I didn't see you."

"So, is that going to be the story?" he asked with a grin.

She looked confused.

He nodded toward where O'Malley was taking off his black hat and getting into the Jag. The tires squealed as he pulled away from the curb.

When she looked back at him, he saw a definite shimmer of challenge in her green eyes.

"I'm sure I don't know what you're talking about, Mr. Blackwell."

A car pulled up behind her and the driver lay on the horn. Ryder stepped aside to let both into the parking garage, shaking his head as he went.

Carol…Carol…he repeated her name in his mind. Lambert. That's right. Her name was Carol Lambert. Coleman had hired her a couple months back.

It wasn't all that surprising that he'd had trouble remembering her name. Although she'd been present in meetings, she usually sat back from the table in a way that guaranteed he barely noticed her, rarely contributing anything, although he understood from Coleman that she was doing a hell of a job since signing on.

He stepped inside the lobby and went straight to the elevator dedicated to his top-floor offices.

Perhaps he'd have to invite the wild Ms. Lambert into his office to see how hot her personal engine ran.

DAMN, damn, damn. She *so* hadn't made that mistake. Had she?

Seline sat at her desk behind a door she never closed but had closed now, hoping against hope that what had happened earlier would stay outside the office. But even though three hours had passed, and she was just a short time away from knocking off for the day, she knew that

Ryder Blackwell wasn't the forgetting kind. And judging by the hot suggestive look he'd given her, he wasn't the timid kind, either.

Of course, she already knew that. Ryder Blackwell, the sixth in a line of wealthy Blackwells—although she understood that Ryder's grandfather had squandered a great deal of the family's fortune…a fortune that the grandson had spent a great deal of time earning back and then some—was not only touted as one of the city's most eligible bachelors, he was also a notorious ladies' man, never seen with the same woman at two consecutive events.

"It's said that men love the thrill of the chase," he'd said in an interview with *GQ*. "But I think women are equally intrigued by a challenge."

It wasn't all that difficult to see why he rated high with both the ladies and the NY press. Money aside—and that was a big aside—he was the epitome of tall, dark and handsome, with just the right amount of devil in his smooth grin and one deep cheek dimple. His attractiveness had been exactly the reason why she'd steered a wide berth around him. And if she couldn't avoid contact, rather than looking up to meet his gaze, she tucked her chin into her chest and murmured responses that he had to ask her to repeat.

Then she'd gone and challenged him to a street race in the middle of Manhattan.

The telephone at her elbow rang. Seline froze and then she forced herself to answer.

"Yes, Rita?"

"Ms. Lambert, Mr. Blackwell says he'd like to see you before you leave for the day."

"Here?"

"No. He'd like you to go up to his office. Just ring his assistant when you're ready so she can signal the elevator."

Seline sighed. "Thanks, Rita."

Signal the elevator.

Oh, she'd known the layout of the building like the back of her hand before she'd ever set foot in it. Architectural plans were easy enough to access. But she'd never had reason to venture into Ryder Blackwell's professional domain. And she didn't want a reason to now. Not with such a short time remaining before a punch of a button would transfer a significant amount from Blackwell & Blackwell's business accounts into a series of dummy front accounts and eventually make its way, untraceably, into her own.

She could pretend she hadn't got the message. Blame the miscommunication on Rita. After all, who she was—or rather wasn't—and why she was really here would become painfully obvious soon enough.

She swiveled restlessly in her chair. This was exactly the reason she'd established a strict set of rules to work by. And today the breaking of one of them had snowballed into the breaking of Golden Rule Number 1: Stay under the radar of the higher-ups.

And in this con they didn't come any higher than Ryder Blackwell.

She clicked through the documents on her computer, then made a couple of notes. There was no way in hell she was going up to that office.

Seline remembered his sexy grin and her panties grew tighter. A reaction that had nothing to do with July sunshine and fast cars, and everything to do with sex and a great candidate to have some with.

2

"UH OH. I know that look."

Ryder turned his leather chair from the clear view he had of the Empire State Building from the forty-fifth floor of the building his company owned. He considered his second-in-command and longtime best friend, John Coleman. "What look?"

Coleman sat back in the righthand guest chair and gave him a wry expression of his own. "That one that says you're about to do something dangerous. Or stupid. Or both."

Ryder grinned, not so much at his friend, but at himself. "I don't know whether I should take offense or be amused."

"Oh, God. You *are* about to do something stupid and dangerous, aren't you?"

"When have I ever done something stupidly dangerous?"

"Oh, how about that impromptu trip to Alaska

two months ago to drop from a helicopter and
snowboard down some virgin mountain when we
had a meeting to close the deal with Trump? Or
the month before that when you disappeared so
you could hike up the side of the Montserrat
volcano before it was due to erupt?"

"You call that dangerous?"

"I definitely call that dangerous."

Ryder leaned forward in his chair. "That's
because risk to you is whether or not to wear
the pink tie your new wife gave you for Valen-
tine's Day."

"Yes, well, someone's got to keep their wits
about them around here."

Ryder's mind wandered to the clock. Four-thirty.

"So what are you considering now?"

"What?"

"Isn't there a hurricane due to hit Florida's
east coast? Are you having your surfboard
waxed?"

"Nothing quite so unimaginative."

"But you *are* considering something."

Ryder picked up his pen and tapped it on his
desk. "Maybe."

It all depended on one very inscrutable Carol
Lambert.

Granted, he'd been privileged to enjoy the

company of a lot of women in his life. And he knew that outer wrappings often were deceiving. There was the raunchy pop star he'd gone out with who had pretended to be an exhibitionist sex kitten in public, but the minute he got her home she'd folded in on herself then passed out from the stress of having to put on such an act all night. He recalled having waited around until morning in that case, convinced the sex—when he got it—would be worth it. But it hadn't been. One-on-one she'd been shy and hesitant, the exact opposite of the image she portrayed for everyone else.

Then there was the icy socialite he'd briefly— very briefly—considered marriage material. She headed the right charities, boasted the right pedigrees and was the perfect hostess of myriad social events. But behind closed doors she was a borderline nymphomaniac. She had nearly shredded his back with her nails and broken his eardrums with her loud and X-rated demands of what she wanted him to do to her for what had to be a record-breaking ten hours straight.

It had been the one and only time that Ryder had been more preoccupied with whether he'd survive what his sex partner might do to him than with the sex itself.

Then there was Carol Lambert.

He leaned back in his chair, ignoring his friend.

There was something about Carol. Something different. The first thing being that the hot lady who'd challenged him to race didn't seem to fit her name, forget the person she turned into the minute she entered the front doors of Blackwell & Blackwell. He'd even consulted her employment records to try to solve the mystery, but nothing from her file had helped him to reconcile the two women with whom he was acquainted. *Acquainted* being the operative word.

And something he hoped to upgrade to *having intimate knowledge* of when she came to his office that afternoon.

"Should I call legal and make sure your insurance policies are up to date?" Coleman asked.

"What insurance policies?"

Coleman stared at him.

Ryder chuckled and got to his feet. "Go home to that pretty wife of yours, John, and stop being such a worrywart. You sound like a nagging mother." He smacked his hand against his friend's back on their way toward the door.

"Promise me you won't do anything I wouldn't do."

Ryder raised a brow.

John sighed. "Okay, then. Promise you'll be careful."

"I'm always careful."

"Why doesn't that make me feel any better?"

The minute John was on his way down the hall to his own office, Ryder's secretary approached.

"There were three calls for you while you were occupied." She said, offered up the message slips.

"Hold on to them, Mrs. Newman. I've got a meeting to make."

"Meeting?" she asked his departing back. "I have no meeting on your agenda."

Ryder grinned at her as he turned inside the elevator then pressed the button for the floor he wanted. "It just came up."

IT TOOK a bit of doing, but Seline managed to push everything up by twelve hours. Which meant that the minute she stepped out of her office, the con would be done and she would be free to shuck Carol Lambert's conservative suits and identity for good.

It also meant that her personal accounts would be that much fatter, while Blackwell & Blackwell's accounts would be that much slimmer.

And, ultimately, it meant that she could duck out before anyone would miss her. Specifically, Ryder Blackwell.

Of course, it went without saying that she also wouldn't have an excuse to see whether or not Ryder growled in bed as satisfyingly as the engine of his car did on the road.

But that was part of the price she paid in her line of work. It came with the territory. Even if the rules she lived by didn't already make involvement with anyone personally connected to any company she targeted off limits, it just made plain business sense to keep her attention focused on the job rather than indulging sexual fantasies that would only endanger her and the con. No matter how delicious the temptation.

And Ryder Blackwell was the epitome of delicious and temptation.

She'd been around long enough to understand that if she were lucky there would be only a handful of men she would connect with in a way that transcended your run-of-the-mill attraction. And she'd felt that connection strongly with Ryder upon realizing who he was when he'd blocked her access to the garage. Within a nanosecond, his gaze had communicated an understanding, an awareness, to her that sometimes years with another person couldn't accomplish. An "I see you" gaze that left her feeling…no, *knowing* that he had seen her. Not the details. Not what her favorite color was or what she was up to. But, rather, more fundamental elements. Almost as if the past, present and future had melted together to become immaterial in light of their meeting, their connection.

Oh, well. While it was certainly the first time she'd had such an experience with a mark, she had the feeling it likely wouldn't be the last. And, probably sooner than she currently believed, she'd forget all about his electric-blue eyes and dimpled cheek and the surge of her blood every time she'd thought about him that afternoon, and use the money she'd stolen from him to further more important plans.

She stuffed the last of the items that could be connected to her inside the cavernous depths of her Louis Vuitton bag and wiped her prints from the drawer she'd closed.

"Going somewhere?"

Seline froze at the sound of Ryder's voice. Somewhere in the back of her mind she gave herself a pat on the back for not having jumped. Even if his sudden presence was definitely of the jump variety.

Not that she hadn't half expected him to show up at her office, despite his request through official channels to see her in his. Mostly because of that connection she'd shared with him. She'd instantly sensed that—not unlike herself—he was someone used to getting what he wanted. And he wanted her.

Her. The woman in the car who'd challenged him to a race. Not Carol Lambert. Although she had to remind herself that he didn't know there was difference. A vast and damaging difference.

It had been that knowing that had prompted her to finish up her business and get out of here posthaste.

Unfortunately, she'd been two minutes too late.

Seline turned her chair to face him in the doorway, giving him her best Carol Lambert tucked-chin smile. "Hello, Mr. Blackwell. I was just getting ready to come up to see you."

"Why do I get the impression you were getting ready to leave instead?"

She tried to act surprised, but she made the mistake of meeting his stimulating gaze. And the challenge there left her incapable of ignoring the desire to rise to it.

So he thought he could handle her, did he?

Thought he knew who she was and by extension thought himself up to the task of tussling with her without consequence?

She found herself smiling.

She had two weaknesses. One was for a good, clean, risky con; the other was proving to a powerful bachelor like Ryder Blackwell how powerless he truly was when it came to a woman like her.

And while she should pass on this one, she found she didn't want to.

All cons came with their risks. And so far this one had run like clockwork. Boringly like clockwork. Maybe a tryst with Ryder was just what was needed to spice it up a little bit.

"Was there something you needed to discuss with me?" she asked, getting up from her desk and coming to stand in front of him.

She watched him watch her approach. His black pupils dilated slightly as his gaze dropped first to her baggy blouse as if searching for the lacy bra underneath, then to her legs, which she knew were killer even in the low-heeled, unappealing shoes she wore.

Seline leaned forward, brushing her breasts against his chest. She had to give him credit for standing still, not giving away with a blink or an intake of breath that her actions surprised him. She picked up a file on the side table behind him, then broke contact as she put it into her bag.

"There are several things I'd like to discuss with you, Ms. Lambert."

She put her bag on the table then reached for her suit jacket hanging on the back of the door. He took it from her and she easily turned so he could help her into it. If his movements were a little more languid than the occasion called for, if his fingers lingered a little too long at the collar, against the burning skin of her neck, she wasn't going to let him see her reaction. Even though she sensed that he knew. Just as she knew that he wanted to touch her in far more intimate ways.

"I only have a few minutes," she said, turning back to face him. "I have a meeting to get to."

His gaze swept up from her neck over her chin to her lips. "Cancel it."

She smiled in a way designed to transmit that he'd just tipped his hand. "Surely whatever is on your mind can wait until morning?"

Until she was long gone and he would begin the process of discovering exactly what she'd been doing while she'd been there. And that it had nothing to do with sex and everything to do with money.

"Actually, it can't. Have dinner with me."

She picked up her bag and edged the handle up to rest over her shoulder. "Dinner? Sounds personal. Doesn't that violate the company's no-fraternization rule?"

The right side of his mouth budged upward, revealing the single dimple that made her tongue tingle with the desire to taste it. "I'll put it on my agenda to change that rule first thing in the morning. One of the benefits of being the boss."

Seline couldn't resist leaning closer to him. The new proximity filled her senses with a scent of lime that made her mouth water further. She dropped her voice to a provocative whisper. "Yes, but that still leaves the rule in effect for tonight. And seeing as I'm a new employee, I wouldn't want to do anything to endanger my position. You know, like having sex with the boss."

"Who said anything about sex?"

She tilted her head so that she was looking into his eyes. "You did. And do. Every time you look at me."

"Astute woman."

"Shameless man."

His chuckle sent a shiver skidding over her hypersensitive nerve endings. It had been a long, long time since mere conversation with a man had made her wet. But if the dampness between her thighs was anything to go by, Ryder had accomplished exactly that.

"Look, Mr. Blackwell—"

"Ryder."

"No matter what guarantees you make, the truth is that sleeping with the boss is never a good idea. Chances are you'll come in tomorrow morning having regretted our...intimacy." She watched as he swallowed thickly. "And then where would I be? Aside from sharing the title of one-night stand with no doubt countless other women in the company?"

"I don't sleep with employees."

"But isn't that what you're proposing now?"

His grin widened. "No. I'm offering dinner."

Seline shivered again and clamped her thighs tightly together, reveling in the luscious sensations rolling through her. "Nothing more?"

"Let's just say that the rest...well, I'll be offering. It's up to you whether or not you take me up on it."

She blinked slowly then smiled. "Your car or mine?"

3

RED-HOT. Reckless. Dangerous.

Ryder couldn't be sure where the danger part came in. All he knew was that the instant they entered the elevator in his Upper East Side building, Carol Lambert stopped playing coy and began playing hard. Not hard to get, but hardball—letting him know exactly what she was after. Which happened to be the same thing he was after. But despite his time with the nympho social-ite, he wasn't accustomed to this unabashed display of carnal desire. Or his own feral response to it.

Carol shoved him against the mirrored back wall of the elevator, kissing him hungrily even as she pushed his suit jacket over his shoulders. One of her legs edged between his, her upper thigh pressing boldly against his erection.

Ryder rolled her so she was the one against the wall, pulling open her blouse to reveal the sexy garments underneath. The black lace should have surprised him, but it didn't. Rather he experienced a sense of relief that the woman he'd raced on the street was evident in the racy underwear. No pretend sex kitten here. She was one hundred percent the real thing.

He grasped her right breast, pressing the circle of her areole more tightly against the lacy cup, then fastened his mouth over the fabric and the flesh beneath, drawing both deeply inside even as he worked his own leg between hers, raising his upper thigh until it met with her crotch. Bracing himself, he lifted her until she slid up the mirror. Her knee-length skirt bunched around her lush hips, revealing that she wore no stockings and that the black thong she had on was all lace.

He groaned, holding her against the wall with one hand even as he lowered to his knees, at eye level with the decadent undergarment. Dipping a finger inside the edge, he tugged the lace aside until her gloriously bare swell of flesh was exposed to his hungry gaze.

His vast experience with women left little doubt as to her arousal. Her labia were swollen, making her sex appear like a fresh fruit just waiting to be plucked. He blew lightly and watched as the skin reacted, contracting so that the pink bit of delicate flesh between her folds peeked out, tempting his tongue.

And it was his tongue he offered.

Carol moaned even as the elevator climbed up the thirty floors. He ran the length of his tongue against the slit, then flicked it over and around her clit, pulling the bud deep into his mouth. Her hands left his hair as she braced herself against the wall. Ryder took in her provocative, half-lidded expression even as he drank deeply of her.

The scent of feminine musk, the sound of her shallow, ragging breathing, filled his senses, increasing his desire for this woman who tasted like fresh peaches and cream but was as naughty as the day was long.

He grasped her right leg and positioned it over his left shoulder, then followed suit with her left leg over his right shoulder. She quickly joined her ankles behind his neck, balancing herself against the mirror even as he dove in for another taste of her.

He was aware of her impending release and moved to delay it, moving his attention from the bud to the blooming entrance just below. So slick. So tight. He lapped her slowly, purposefully. As soon as he heard her breathing even out a bit, he traveled back up to the fleshy button and fastened his lips around it again, sucking deeply.

She came apart instantly, her legs tightening, her cry echoing against the elevator walls at the same time an electronic ding sounded.

Ryder thought she might panic at the thought that someone might see them. Instead she rode out the wave of her orgasm then collapsed against the wall, making quite the provocative image with her wild hair, her skirt bunched around her waist, her legs still crossed around his neck as he looked up at her.

She smiled at him languidly. "My, Mr. Blackwell, you do appear to have your skills."

He chuckled as he freed her legs. She found her footing and he rose to stand next to her.

The elevator doors slid open to reveal his warmly lit, empty penthouse. During the drive home—they'd taken their separate cars—he'd called his butler Jonathon, asking for discretion. A silver ice bucket holding a bottle of champagne, a tray of chocolate-tipped strawberries and a bowl of cream and the soft strains of old Motown melodies were the only evidence that Jonathan was anywhere in residence.

"After you," Ryder said.

FOR JUST one night Seline wanted to forget the past…forget the future. She wanted to live in this one moment, and this one moment alone.

She'd need all the help she could get. Because both the past and the future were difficult to ignore for even one night.

She looked around. She'd always appreciated a man with good taste. And Ryder obviously had it in spades.

Languidly strolling into the penthouse, hyper-aware of every nerve ending in her body, the chafing of her nipples against her bra, the throbbing of her womanhood, she took in the mammoth living and dining area, colorfully yet sparsely decorated. Probably it had been put together by an interior decorator. She snatched a strawberry from a tray and bit down on the succulent fruit even as she moved to consider a small framed Manet over an antique, ivory-inlaid banquet. A very good decorator who had taken Ryder into consideration during the planning process.

And likely Ryder had taken the decorator right on the huge ottoman that served as a coffee table between two long sofas.

She shivered.

It had been so long since she'd indulged herself with casual sex. So long that she felt her emotions exaggerating the not-unfamiliar sensations. Her elevator orgasm just as the compartment had stopped moving had rocked her to the marrow. Even now, she was uber-aware of every move Ryder made even though her back was to him.

A crystal flute was placed in front of her. She put it down on the buffet then scooted to sit on the surface, spreading her legs wantonly.

"Nice place."

Usually when she made a comment like that, the person in question took a look around as if seeing through her eyes. Not Ryder. He trapped her gaze with his and didn't blink, secure in the knowledge that it *was* a nice place. And that it had nothing at all to do with the reason she was there.

"Thank you."

He put his flute down on the other side of her, his gaze dropping to where her blouse bowed open, then lower still to her bared thighs.

"Are you hungry?" he murmured.

"Mmm." She caught the waist of his slacks and yanked him forward, his suit jacket long since discarded by the door.

Then she set about showing him exactly what she was hungry for.

Many women she knew sorely underestimated the importance of a good kiss. And oh, did, Ryder

Blackwell know how to kiss. His lips were firm yet malleable, his mouth damp but not too wet. And he didn't go for her tonsils as other men she'd known over the years had made the mistake of doing. Instead he lingered with his lips on hers, his mouth not quite open, not quite closed, his tongue dipping out briefly before he finished the kiss.

Seline grew aware of her shortness of breath. That and he hadn't touched her beyond their kiss since they'd entered the penthouse.

She scooted forward on the buffet, her softness instantly meeting his pants-covered hardness. She briefly bit on her bottom lip, an ache the size of Manhattan gaping within her. An ache that only he could satisfy.

His hands squeezed her legs near her knees then slid up. Her instinct was to throw her head back and allow him to do what he would.

Which was why she instead caught his hands, slid down from the table, then led him toward the wide, open staircase to their right. Swaying her hips suggestively, she climbed three or four steps, aware of the view he was being afforded from the back. She felt a hand on her ass and she paused, allowing the hot branding to ripple through her. Then he was pulling her toward him, forcing her to lie against the carpeted steps as he fitted himself between her thighs.

Seline groaned, welcoming his weight as she pulled at his tie and shirt, then abandoned both for the fastener to his slacks. He hungrily kissed her as she tugged his zipper down, working her hand inside his boxers until the scalding length of him filled her palm.

While their clothed fondling had left her with little doubt as to his size, it had masked how very impressive he was. She idly measured his length, finding him going well beyond the stretch of her fingers and palm together. She encircled the turgid flesh, finding that she could barely touch thumb to fingertips.

Mmm…

Seline's mouth watered with the desire to taste the silken flesh. She trailed her hand down the thick shaft, feeling his heartbeat at the root, her own heart beating hard against her chest in awareness of his reaction to her touch.

He reached for his back pocket and took out a condom while she worked his slacks down his hips, then he rid himself of the constricting material. Next was her skirt, his shirt, her blouse, his briefs, until finally they lay against the steps completely nude, the glass wall on the other side of the stairs reflecting the golden globe of the sun beginning to set off to the west. Seline helped him sheath his erection then arched her back in preparation for his entry.

Instead, he grasped her chin in his right hand, holding her still as he deeply kissed her.

Seline blinked open her eyes. Her chest contracted to the point of pain and she lost her breath.

She immediately labeled the sensation. She'd felt it only one other time. And back then it had been much more about intimacy than sex.

And she wanted strictly sex.

She switched her attention from his face to his shoulder, biting lightly as she wriggled free of his grasp and turned, climbing a couple of more steps then arching her back, presenting him with a carnal view she knew no man could resist.

She knew a moment of disappointment when he followed where she led, grasping her hips as he positioned himself from behind. But that emotion was banished to the winds as he fit the head of his penis against her opening then thrust into her to the hilt.

All coherent thought left her, and sheer sensation quickly filled the void, pressing outward until she was afraid she wouldn't be able to contain it.

So good…

He rocked against her, his sac swaying against her swollen womanhood, then withdrew, his right hand circling her hip to find the bit of flesh and give it a pinch. Seline threw back her head and moaned as he thrust again, and again, causing her bare breasts to sway, her sensitive nipples repeatedly grazing the carpeted step beneath them. His strokes grew from controlled to more frenzied as Seline bore back against him, longing for an even deeper penetration. She reached down between her legs, gently grasping his balls and coaxing him to slow his movements. Whenever he thrust, she rubbed the globes against her slick flesh, shivering at the sensation, then released so he could withdraw.

All too quickly she could no longer concentrate on the move and dropped her hand. The instant she did, he increased the frequency and urgency of his thrusts.

Flesh slapped against flesh, moans competed against groans…

Then finally she was toppling over the other side of the virtual staircase out over a vista she hadn't seen in a very long time, everything shaded in red.

SELINE lay back against the Egyptian cotton sheets. She was naked, she was spent and she was having a hard time concentrating on anything other than the delicious throbbing in her various body parts. Patches of stubble burn marred her inner thighs, her breasts and her chin. She had rug burn on her knees and elbows from the stairs. Her nipples protested when she tried to drape the top sheet over them, so she left them bare as she listened to the sound of the shower in the other room.

The purple-hued world outside the tall, floor-to-ceiling windows told her dawn would soon break. And that it was way past time to hightail it out of here. It wouldn't be too long before Coleman got to the office and discovered what she had done. While she'd built in certain mechanisms to delay the discovery, she knew Coleman was no fool and that he was also the type of dependable guy who would check account activity every morning.

She glanced toward the clock on the nightstand, finding a pillow covering it. Seline dragged it off and the clock fell with it. She picked it up from the floor.

Five forty-five. Damn.

She could count the times she'd had such great sex on two fingers. With Joey Caprioti when she was nineteen and just coming to know her own sexuality. And now.

She smiled stupidly. Yes, Ryder Blackwell was

definitely no slouch in bed. She'd known men who were roaring lions in the boardroom but lazy cats in the bedroom. Not Ryder. He was as ambitious between the sheets as he was outside them. Sheets being optional.

In fact, they hadn't hit the bed until sometime after 3:00 a.m. And only then because they'd risked serious injury in the kitchen when he'd hoisted her onto the counter and knocked over a stand of butcher knives.

The shower shut off.

Seline bounced up from the bed, collected her clothes, then headed at a run for the door.

No matter how good, no sex was worth the risk of a long prison sentence.

4

WHEN RYDER had emerged from his shower to find Carol gone, he'd been amused. He'd hoped the sound of the water would wake her and entice her to slip under the multi-jet spray with him.

Instead she'd left.

When she hadn't shown up to work by ten, he suspected she'd gone back to her place and fallen asleep. He thought maybe she'd be in later.

Then around eleven, John Coleman had requested an emergency meeting.

By 4:00 p.m. Ryder was furiously aware of everything one Carol Lambert had done. Only it hadn't been Carol Lambert but the sexy woman he'd slept with last night. Because Carol Lambert was a thirty-eight-year-old brunette who still lived in Washington State and hadn't transferred to New York and his company, but rather was taking extended time off to have her first child.

"How much are we looking at?" he asked Coleman.

"Three quarters of a mil."

Ryder sat back in his chair as if hit in the chest with a punching bag.

"This woman was good. She brokered a deal between Blackwell and a sham company that as of this morning no longer exists."

"Get the money back."

"Easier said than done. The instant the money hit the sham company's account it was then automatically transferred out to various other accounts, and I'm guessing even more accounts from there. The minute the money left our bank it essentially became untraceable." Coleman shook his head as he considered the printouts he held. "This woman was a pro. She knew exactly what she was doing." He looked up. "Johnstone says this was a set-up from the get go. She borrowed the Lambert woman's résumé, burrowed deep into the company, then meticulously set us up."

Ryder rubbed his face, as much to wake himself up from the nightmare he was in the middle of as to rid himself of the erotic images that kept sliding through his mind from last night.

Coleman didn't know he'd spent the night

sleeping with the enemy. Sleeping—hah! They hadn't slept at all. He'd had Carol, the con artist, every which way it was possible to have a woman. Hell, he'd had more sex with her in one night than he'd had in the entire year.

And he'd been stupid enough to believe he'd be getting more of it.

And still wanted it despite what she'd done.

"Johnstone's got nearly every detective firm in Manhattan working the case now."

"So he's confident she'll be caught."

Coleman grimaced. "Look, Ry, I've never been one to mislead you. The truth is, given the professional nature of the crime, with every moment that passes the trail gets colder."

"You mean there's a chance we won't catch up with her?"

"More than a chance. A probability."

Coleman's cell phone rang, and he answered. A minute later, he rang off.

"The apartment she rented came furnished and was in Carol Lambert's name. And it was wiped clean. Not a print anywhere. But they think they got a couple of hair samples."

"Security cameras?"

"The staff is going over Blackwell's videos now. But routine dictates that they erase tapes after a twenty-four-hour period so all we'll have is the footage from yesterday."

Ryder looked at his watch. The woman had left his place just before six. Nine hours ago. Which meant she could be pretty much anywhere in the world by now. Probably collecting the cash she'd stolen from his company.

"I want to see the footage as soon as it comes in."

"I don't expect to get much," Coleman said. "She always walked as if staring at something on her shoe. I thought it was because she was self-conscious, but now we know the real reason."

Ryder also knew the real reason she'd originally rebuffed his advances yesterday after finding out he'd been the one she'd raced with. No doubt number one in the con artist's handbook was "Fly under the radar."

"Ryder?"

He blinked at Coleman.

"Are you okay?"

No. He was far from okay. Because he was all too aware that if he hadn't taken the woman back to his place last night, he wouldn't be obsessed with the situation right now. He'd have left everything in Coleman's capable hands and gone on with his day full of meetings overseeing expansion plans, financial realignments and mergers. While the amount of money wasn't anything to sneeze at by any means, it wasn't enough to warrant the type of attention he was giving to it. The company lost that amount in a day if truck drivers went on strike in the Midwest.

Despite all that, he'd cancelled everything, mentally incapable of doing anything but concentrating on this one thing. This was personal.

"I want to talk to Johnstone," he said, naming the head of security.

"I can do that. Don't you have a meeting regarding Stanton?"

Ryder got up from his chair and put his suit jacket on. "I cancelled it."

"But we're in the final stages of closing the deal. Everything's set to go into motion the instant the takeover papers are signed. Do you think that's a good idea?"

No, it was a decidedly bad idea. The not-altogether-friendly leveraged buyout of his second-largest competitor would give him a marketing edge in the nation's distribution system, one of the many areas in which Blackwell & Blackwell owned businesses. But Ryder couldn't help himself. He was going to find this woman

who'd impersonated Carol Lambert, the woman
in the rented Audi, and he was going to find her
now.

BY THE END of the week, Ryder had been forced
to accept that his finding her wasn't going to be
easily checked off his agenda.

It was a Sunday and along with Blackwell &
Blackwell's own security team, he was paying three
detective firms double their going rate to find her.

Only it was beginning to look like no amount of
money was going to be able to uncover the true
identity of the woman who'd screwed him... twice.

Coleman told him that perhaps it was time to
admit defeat and move on. Besides, the company
could write the loss off. There was the Stanton
deal in limbo and very possibly in danger of un-
raveling altogether. But Ryder couldn't seem to
think of anything else.

"Are you all right, son?"

Ryder looked at his father, walking next to
him along the Coney Island boardwalk. The place
where he'd grown up, but now only visited when
he saw his father every other Sunday.

"That's the third time you've asked me," Ryder
said, shoving his hands into the pockets of his
Lauren khakis.

Growing up, he'd heard countless times how much he and his father looked alike. Some of the family's relatives had even taken to calling him Junior, though his father's name was Alan. But time had erased those physical similarities. And while Ryder only lived across the river in Manhattan, it might as well have been across the Atlantic as far as their lifestyles went. His father would take the train into town every now and again for coffee and to go to a museum exhibit or an off-off-Broadway show, but otherwise their lives were separate. And had been since Ryder's mother had died of breast cancer fifteen years ago.

Of course, it didn't help that their differences extended to their own personal ideologies.

Being born a Blackwell, his father had once told him, was no different than being born under any other name, despite the historical and cultural significance it once held in New York. Ryder would always remember that conversation, held when he'd come home soaked on a rainy Tuesday in April. He was nine and he'd just learned that his ancestors had been instrumental in the building of Manhattan and that even his grandfather, his father's father, had enjoyed great wealth, until the mid 1950s when the family had been bankrupted.

His father? His take was that it had probably happened for a good reason. While Alan Blackwell had been educated at Harvard and enjoyed a privileged upbringing, he'd adjusted amazingly well to his new station in life. In fact, it seemed to suit him better, his mother used to say. Rather than working as the CEO of the family company and attending Broadway openings and Lincoln Center charity events, he'd taught American Lit at NYU for most of his career, and had just recently retired, speaking here and there when invited.

Otherwise he lived a quiet life in Brooklyn, visiting his favorite bakery every morning, reading the newspaper, or with his nose in whatever obscure book he'd picked up from the used bookstore on the corner.

But whereas his father had experienced life on both sides of the fence, young Ryder had spent his youth with his fingers fused to the fence links, staring longingly at the skyline across the river. Driven not only to recover his family's longstanding wealth and status, but to up the ante on both counts.

And at thirty-six he'd done all that and more.

"And that's the third time you haven't answered me." His father chuckled quietly then put his arm around his son's shoulders. "Ask the experienced, not the learned."

Ryder offered a half grin. His life had been filled with quotes from one source or another. Mostly his father had been trying to convince him that it wasn't how much he had in his pockets but the love he held in his heart that was the true measure of a good man.

Ryder had in turn spent most of his life ignoring that advice.

"Just some things going on at work," he said.

"Anything you'd like to share?"

"No, no."

"And here I thought the problem might be a woman." The senior Blackwell drew to a stop near the edge of the boardwalk and squinted out at the sparkling Atlantic. "You know, one of your mother's biggest regrets was that she never got to enjoy a grandchild."

"If I remember correctly, you were the one to say that I probably would never have children."

"That's because you have to find a good woman first. And you move too fast to catch bad women, much less good ones." He looked at him. "Up until recently I at least hoped you'd make an effort at continuing the Blackwell name if just for legacy's sake."

"I thought you didn't buy into any of that."

"I don't. But you do. Me? I'd just like to have a grandson or granddaughter who I can teach to play chess. Or at least know that my son, my only child, will finally learn what it means to know love."

"I know love. I had it with Mom. With you."

"And when I'm gone?"

Ryder also stared out at the ocean. "Are you planning on a trip I don't know about?"

"No. But it's something that's been on my mind a lot lately."

"I told you it was a bad idea when you retired—"

"I was forced out, Ryder. There's nothing more irritating than a rambling old man who can't find his notes."

"So teach somewhere here. At a Brooklyn school."

"My teaching days are over." They began walking again. "Besides, if I couldn't teach my own son, tell me what impact I'd really have on other's children."

It wasn't like his father to talk about death in such a direct way. And Ryder wasn't sure how to take it. While he'd heard other parents talk to their children about the impending visit from the Grim Reaper, even if that visit was some twenty to thirty years in the future, his father had never been like that. There were too many topics to discuss, politics to cut through.

"A wiser man, perhaps, might have figured out early on that the way to teach you was to misteach you."

"How do you mean?"

"If I had encouraged you, no insisted on, you rebuilding the family fortune, you would have rebelled and done the opposite. Had I told you having a wife and children would only saddle you down, you probably would be married fifteen years now with three kids."

Ryder chuckled. "Reverse psychology. But you're leaving out that I would have seen through such a ruse. Besides, you could never have done it. It goes against everything you are. Everything you taught me to be."

"But you're still not married."

"Why don't you travel, Pops? You and mom always talked about wanting to travel."

In fact, he'd arranged a month-long tour of England, Scotland and Ireland while his mother was still well enough to travel.

"I'm too old for the hassle. Besides, that was your mom's and my dream. Without her...well, without her it wouldn't be the same."

And one day, perhaps soon, Ryder would be faced with life without his father in it. And for the first time he accepted that it wouldn't be the same, either.

5

THE FOLLOWING FRIDAY everyone around Ryder had officially admitted defeat. But Ryder refused to raise the white flag.

He stood at the windows of his office staring out from his elevated spot at the buildings of Manhattan spread out before him like a giant's handful of mismatched dice. Somewhere out there was the woman who had set his sheets on fire, then outwitted him. And he intended to find her. Whatever it took.

He turned back to his desk and the telephone book he had opened to with the listing of detective agencies in the tri-borough area. Being in Brooklyn with his father last weekend had given him a couple of ideas by reminding him that he hadn't always been standing at the top of the mountain. He'd gotten a raw view from the gutters looking up, as well. After a four-year stint in the marines, he'd received his degree from

Columbia, then had emerged onto the social scene using his family name as his passport with which to rebuild the Blackwell empire. Within six years, he'd sat at the helm of the first company at which he'd worked. Two years after that, he'd bought the company and taken it private and had been expanding the business ever since.

And he hadn't gotten where he was now without getting his hands dirty from time to time. And the mystery woman made him want to thrust both hands directly into the black dirt.

Ryder noted the name and address of a Brooklyn detective agency then picked up the phone. Sometimes it took a fellow gutter rat to find another one in the maze that was the criminal underworld. He picked up the phone and placed the call.

THE BROOKLYN detective agency was little more than a small storefront that could have easily have been a travel agency or a take-out restaurant, not unlike the other businesses around it. The furniture was old, but the place was clean. And P.I. Kylie Capshaw had the tough exterior of someone who'd spent more than a few years foraging around in the gutters, both as a result of the hand life had dealt her, as well as to succeed as a woman in her chosen profession.

"Mr. Blackwell. A pleasure." She said, extended her hand.

"Ryder, please," he said, returning her firm shake. She was dressed in jeans and a T-shirt and well-worn cowboy boots he suspected were steel-toed and capable of doing a fair amount of damage should anyone cross her. And she looked like the type who wouldn't hesitate to do that damage.

"Slumming it, huh?" she questioned, taking two mugs out of a metal desk drawer then crossing to a coffeemaker.

Ryder glanced at his Lagerfeld suit. He hadn't thought about changing his clothes to take the late-afternoon meeting. "In a manner of speaking."

"So tell me," she said, sitting down behind the old metal desk covered with paperwork. She took a bottle of Bailey's from a different drawer then poured the Irish cream into the coffee and handed him a cup. Ryder took it then watched as she sipped hers. "How do you think I'll be able to help you where others haven't been able to? Because I get the feeling that you're not here for a personal matter you don't want others to know about. Am I right?"

"Spot on."

"Who've you been to?"

He told her.

"Ah. The Big Three." She raised her brows. "And they haven't been able to get what you want?"

"No. While this is a white-collar crime, a blue-collar criminal committed it."

"And your reasoning is that it takes a blue-collar gal to find a blue-collar criminal."

Her words weren't so much as a question as they were a statement. "Yes," Ryder answered simply.

Kylie grinned. "Then it looks like you've come to the right place…."

BETWEEN Seline's legs vibrated one of the most powerful machines built by man, and something she'd been craving ever since sneaking out of Ryder Blackwell's bed the week before. The custom black Ducati 999R Xerox motorcycle with a Testastretta 143-hp engine gave her a sense of freedom not even a car could afford her. And as she ran it down the empty roads in rural southwest Wisconsin, the roar drowning out all other sounds, the air whipping around her black leather-clad body, she felt like a hellcat demon on a mission.

That is, if she ignored that there was no real mission, to rid the brand of Ryder's touch from her skin.

It had been nine days since she'd pulled one

of the biggest cons of her career. Yet a sense of a job incomplete tailed her like a state trooper with his siren blaring. Returning home usually calmed her, allowed her distance from her last job in order to concentrate on what needed to be done to ensure her security and to focus on the next con. But not this time. This time, her mind cease-lessly returned to Blackwell & Blackwell. Or more specifically to the man who sat at the helm.

She popped the clutch and further gunned the engine, nudging the speedometer needle up past a hundred.

Her father Angelo had once told her that grifters subconsciously knew when their time was up. That they sense when they'd made a fatal mistake, then come home to find the authorities waiting for them. But somehow she didn't think that was the case here. While she'd had to push up the timeline of her con by a day, and had left a couple of loose ends dangling, she and the money were ultimately untraceable.

Which brought her right back to Ryder himself.

There was a really good reason why she never got personally involved on a job, beyond it not being a professionally shrewd move. But she didn't want to think about that. Not now. She wanted to focus on the future instead.

In fact, that's why she was out on this hour-long ride toward Chicago. To clear her mind of the cobwebs draped there by Ryder Blackwell...and the lessons of her past so she could look to tomorrow.

Before long two lanes turned into three then four and Seline was officially on the outskirts of Chicago. She slowed her speed and drove straight downtown, toward a bakery she'd passed during a previous ride that had looked intriguing. After she'd parked, secured her helmet to the bike and straightened her skin-tight leather jacket, she stepped inside Natale's Bakery on Taylor Street. The Italian sweets shop was just what the doctor ordered, if only for the minute it reminded her of home in New York and the family she'd been forced to leave behind there years before.

A frazzled-looking, attractive woman at one of the tables called out, her words mingling with the bell that jangled as Seline entered, "Hey, Izzie. What do you know about computers?"

Seline guessed the curvy woman with long dark-brown hair on the other side of the counter was Izzie.

After acknowledging Seline, she answered the other customer's question, "Well, I don't know how to find any naked pictures of Heath Ledger, and I haven't figured out how to send a death-ray to spammers, but I do the Web site for the bakery."

"I hear ya."

Seline lowered her sunglasses to eye the café's menu.

"So you know how to enlarge pictures?" the woman at the table continued. "Other than ones of naked movie stars?"

Izzie grinned. "Yeah, give me a sec." She looked at Seline. "What can I get you?"

Seline placed her order for an espresso and asked if there were any fresh cannoli.

"Sorry, Lilith took the last."

She looked over her shoulder at the woman getting cannoli crumbs on the laptop she was bent over.

"Will that be all?"

Seline nodded and paid her then, watching as she came out from behind the counter to stand next to the other woman.

"What do you need?" she asked.

Lilith jumped at Izzie's sudden appearance, and then laughed. Seline understood the response. She'd been living on the edge for so long, any loud sound threatened to push her over the side.

"I need a close-up of this guy's ring."

Izzie leaned toward the computer and squinted. "It's pretty big already."

"Not big enough."

Izzie sat down and slid the laptop toward her. Seline stepped imperceptibly closer, watching as Izzie's fingers flew over the keypad with confident ease, but when she turned the screen back toward the other woman the picture was distorted, connected blobs with no detail.

"That won't work," Lilith said.

Izzie shrugged. "You need a higher resolution picture."

Her friend grunted. "How can I get a higher resolution picture?"

"Where'd you get the first one?" Seline asked. Computers were second nature to her, her partner in crime in a manner of speaking.

Lilith looked at her. "Newspaper Web site."

"They'd use a lower resolution there so the page will load faster. They'd probably only use high res in the actual printing process."

Lilith frowned. "I don't have any contacts at the paper. I don't think they'd give access to their archives to just anyone."

Seline arched a brow and grinned. "Do you want access?"

"Most definitely."

Seline put her coffee down on the table and threaded her fingers together to give them a stretch. Lilith scooted around to give her room, but she simply leaned over the machine and worked standing up, her eyes darting periodically outside Natale's plate-glass window.

"Nice ride," Lilith commented about the Ducati.

Her fingers didn't slow. "Gets me around. Who is this guy, anyway? Don't tell me you're trying to figure out if that ring is a wedding band and he's the asshole you've been dating for the last three months."

Lilith nearly spat out what Seline guessed was cappuccino. "Ew."

She nodded in approval. "So he's not your lover."

"Say that again and I'll dump the dregs on you. He's a jerk I'm investigating."

"A jerk?" Seline asked. "What makes him different from every other man on this planet?"

"Good question," Izzie muttered. With no other customers in the shop and, Seline guessed, closing time quickly approaching, she'd taken to wiping down the tables of all their remnant stickiness. Lilith looked impatient as Seline accessed a number of remote, unconnected servers and then circled back to what she wanted to do, shielding the laptop from any trace that might be run back to it. She suspected she was being overly cautious, but in her line of business, caution kept you free.

"Name one guy who isn't a jerk," Seline said, swiping her tongue over her lips as her concentration deepened.

"Mac Mancusi," Lilith whispered.

"You know Mac?" Izzie asked, apparently familiar with the name.

Seline mistyped a word and had to correct it, the obviously Italian name distracting her. Maybe returning to the bakery wouldn't be a good idea.

"Biblically," Lilith said.

Izzie's eyebrows shot up. "No kidding? You and Mac? Wow. I can't picture the two of you together."

"You won't need to. We won't be together much longer."

"You're dumping him?" Izzie was clearly disappointed. "You're right, you know, Mac's not a jerk. He grew up just a few blocks from here. Our families know each other. I'd think any woman would love to catch a good, honest cop like him."

Seline stopped her work. "You're sleeping with a cop?"

Lilith pushed the laptop closer. "I'm sleeping

with him, not married to him," she insisted. "Trust me when I say that my definition of right and wrong varies from his by huge degrees. Keep working and your next ten espressos are on me."

Seline definitely couldn't return to the bakery, no matter how good the coffee and cannoli. She covered her uneasiness with a smile and returned to her task. "I won't be around that long, but thanks for the offer."

"Add her to my tab," Lilith instructed Izzie. "Any time she stops in, coffee's on me. What's your name?"

"Seline."

With a nod, Lilith told Izzie to give Seline free rein of her coffee tab.

"Does that mean you're actually going to pay it someday?" Izzie asked, an amused grin tugging at her full lips.

"Soon. I swear."

Lilith tapped her fingers impatiently on the table, stopping when Seline gave her warning glare.

Finally, she cracked the code to access the newspaper's computer—you would think programmers would learn that the word *God* was the first backdoor password a hacker tried—and did a search for photos that fell within the dates of the one Lilith was interested in. "Don't get ahead of yourself. I haven't got it…wait…ding, ding, ding. We have a winner."

Lilith clapped enthusiastically. "I had a feeling you were up to the task."

"You would," Izzie quipped.

Seline stood back, wondering what that meant. She took in Lilith's flowy top and pentagram charm, thinking that she looked a lot like the woman who'd read tarot cards down the street from where she'd grown up.

Lilith appeared to hesitate as she stared at the ring on the man in the photo's hand. She took a deep breath, blowing it out slowly as if willing herself to remain calm.

Seline eyed her. "Is that what you need?"

Lilith saved the image to the hard drive, e-mailed it to someone, and then shut off the machine and tucked it into her bag. "Unfortunately, yes." She stood and extended her hand to Seline, who, after a moment's hesitation, gave it a strong shake. "Thanks for your help. If you ever have need of a psychic, look me up. Well, in a few weeks when I'm back on the job." She patted the laptop case. "I think I just found my golden ticket back to gainful employment. Izzie, thanks for the sugar boost and the wi-fi."

Izzie waved. "Anytime."

Lilith weaved through the tables and chairs until she reached the door. The bell jangled before Izzie called out, "Lilith!"

Lilith turned.

"Don't be so quick to write off a great guy like Mac," Izzie said, her voice tentative, as if she couldn't quite believe she was offering romantic advice. "Maybe you and he can find a way to make it work, even if you think there's no way it ever could."

Humph. Seline had always been one to trust her instincts over her heart. If your gut told you something, you were wise to heed it.

She thought of Ryder and the impossibility of anything working between them and then banished the thought.

"Here," she said, putting a hundred-dollar bill on the counter. "For her tab. I sense that she needs the money more than I do. And I don't have to be psychic to figure that out."

"Thanks." Izzie sounded surprised.

Seline smiled, picked up her coffee and then took that as her cue to leave. Never stay anywhere long enough for them to get to know you. While it sometimes left her longing for something more, she knew she had to make certain tradeoffs in life. And this, unfortunately, was one of hers.

6

AN HOUR and a half later Seline turned onto the long, private drive that wound around five acres of lush, sloping land before finally leading to her house set up on a low hill in the midst of open land, the security gates behind her clanging shut. She set a leisurely pace with the bike, taking in the grounds. A part of her enjoyed the landscape. Another looked for flaws in the security.

Often was the time when she looked around and thought, damn, what a great effin' place. I must be doing pretty good.

This was one of those times. And she hoped soon it would really become home.

She pressed the button to open the fifth and farthest door on her multi-car garage and rode the bike inside, then cut the engine.

"Jeeves?" Seline called out when she entered the house from the garage. There was no answer. She hung her leather coat on a hook and shook out her dark hair…hair that was a shade darker than her regular color as a result of the dye it had taken to cover the bleaching she'd used to impersonate Carol Lambert.

Her steps slowed then stopped altogether when she called out again to no response.

Someone was here…

Seline hugged the wall then reached for the switchblade tucked into the back pocket of her leather pants. A quick flick of her wrist and it was ready to go.

Jeeves was always aware when she returned. It was the noise she made on those occasions, he said. In this case, the sound of her Ducati engine would have been more than enough of a heads-up.

Yet he hadn't responded to her calls.

Shit.

Seline remembered the feeling earlier. Recalled the advice from her father that she'd sense when her time was up. When she'd played her last ace and the law was about to slam down around her.

But even facing the unusual silence of the house, she didn't think that was the case here. And she generally wasn't into self-delusion.

She turned the corner into the kitchen. A pot of water was boiling on the stove. She slunk around the corner into the hall leading to the large foyer. Empty. She stepped out into the open doorway to the sitting room and spotted the reason for the silence.

Ryder Blackwell sat in one of the wing chairs in front of the fireplace, hands casually folded in his lap, his grin telling her he'd been thinking about her at least as much as she'd been thinking about him.

Albeit she'd guess for different reasons....

"HELLO, Carol."

Ryder relaxed in the comfortable chair that would look at home in any one of his three posh residences within the United States. He was exactly where he'd planned to be for the past nine days. Confronting the woman who had conned him in more ways than one. But this time the power was fully in his hands.

"Or should I say Seline?"

Late-afternoon sunlight glinted off the blade she held as she sighed and dropped it to her side.

"Christ, Ryder. What in the hell do you think you're doing?"

He raised a brow as he watched her skillfully close the blade then tuck it into the back pocket of her tight black leather jeans.

Ryder took her in from head to foot. While she

looked nothing like the woman who had worked at his firm or graced his bed, he'd known instantly it was her. Would have known it if it were pitch black and they were in a roomful of people.

Her hair was dark-brown now instead of blond. And the tough biker style suited her in a way that business attire had not.

He hadn't fooled himself into thinking that he understood anything about the woman even now pouring a splash of bourbon into two crystal decanters. The thick thud of her boots sounded against the Aubusson rug as she crossed it and held one of the glasses out for him to take.

She didn't say anything as he accepted it, downing her own. She stared at him, her gray eyes darkened by widening pupils as she wiped the side of her full mouth with the back of her hand then held the tumbler against her white T-shirt-covered chest.

"Jeeves?" she said, focusing her attention on the fireplace mantel rather than on Ryder.

"Yes, ma'am." The man he'd convinced to let him in appeared in the doorway. Even though he was dressed in black pants and a white shirt, Ryder got the impression he would have looked equally as comfortable in a vested butler's suit.

"Bring us a tray."

"Right away, ma'am."

Ryder allowed his attention to drift back to the woman standing within arm's reach. The scent of fine leather teased his nostrils along with a trace of coconut and the outdoors. When he'd first raced her on the streets of Manhattan, he'd had no idea about the woman in the Audi. But after having spent an erotic night with her, he didn't find her appearance now that much of a stretch.

She was a chameleon, changing her colors at will and blending in wherever she went. Surely, it was part of her job. But was he seeing the real Seline Sanborn now? Or was this merely another facet of her diamond-hard shell?

"Do you have any idea what you've done?" she asked quietly.

Ryder considered the glass that he had yet to drink from. "Funny. I'm here to talk about what you've done."

She rested her left hand against the mantel then looked down at him, her expression serious. "I'm going to ask you a question. It's very important how you answer it."

Ryder stared back at her.

"How did you find me?"

"I'm not without my resources."

Seline dropped her head and closed her eyes. "Okay, I conned you, you found me, I'll give your money back. But that's not what's at issue here. I need to know what resources you used to uncover my true identity."

"Like, are the authorities aware of your whereabouts?"

She didn't respond or move. And, oddly, he got the distinct impression that that wasn't what she was talking about.

"Answer me, Ryder. This is more important than you can know."

He didn't say anything, if only because this wasn't exactly the way he'd imagined this going down.

He wasn't sure what he *had* envisioned, but it was closer to her running in the opposite direction or trying to sweet talk him. Not matter-of-factly stating the series of events and offering him his money back as though this was a business meeting, then demanding he answer questions.

He put his glass down on a table and then stood, walking a few paces away to lessen the impact of her nearness.

"I want you to answer a few questions for me first."

She turned toward him, her eyes dark and dangerous. "Shoot."

"Why Blackwell?"

She had her hands behind her back and was leaning casually against the large fireplace. He was reminded that she had a knife in her back pocket. "Why *not* Blackwell?"

"So the hit wasn't personal."

"I learned a long time ago not to mix business with pleasure."

"Then what happened between us was business then."

She smiled. "No, that was pleasure."

Ryder held her gaze.

"The business end of the con was done."

He watched as she pushed from the fireplace and slowly crossed to stand in front of him. She appeared to be staring at something on his shoulder, allowing him to gaze at her face without restraint.

Damn, but she was beautiful. Her skin was flawless, aside from a small scar above her right brow that merely added to her attractiveness rather than detracted from it. She wore little makeup, but her eyes didn't need it, not with lashes as thick as branches and a generous mouth that could fuel enough fantasies to last the rest of his life.

"So now you answer my question," she said, focusing on his eyes. "How did you find me?"

Damn it all to hell, but he still wanted her on a physical level he couldn't ignore. Her proximity brought to life every part of him, left him longing to kiss her lips and snake his arms around her slender waist and pull her tight against him. Take up where they'd left off.

"Where would you like it, ma'am?" Jeeves appeared next to them with a silver tray filled with teacups and scones and clotted cream and jams.

Seline closed her eyes. "Remind me to talk to you about your awful sense of timing, Jeeves."

The butler grinned at her as if he believed his timing was perfect as he put the tray down on the table near the long sofa. "Yes, ma'am."

Just like that they were alone again.

And Ryder became doubly aware of how very close she was.

And did something he definitely hadn't planned to do. At least not consciously.

He kissed her.

THERE WAS a time when Seline might have used sex in order to get what she wanted. A time well before she learned how very dangerous such a prospect could prove.

But it hadn't been her who had initiated the kiss, it had been Ryder. And his mouth on hers felt better, hotter, than any kiss had a right to.

She pressed her palms against his chest to push him away. But when they met the solid wall, her resolve faltered. His tongue against hers, his fingers at the side of her neck, felt so damn good. Within an instant the house around her faded to black, the questions surrounding his presence disappeared, leaving only the sound of his ragged breathing and the thump-thump of her heart.

He groaned. And she pushed him slightly away.

"I thought that was supposed to be my move," she whispered, gazing up at him.

He cracked a grin. "By all means."

She lingered for a moment longer then turned away from him, walking toward the sofa where she sat down and poured the tea. He stood where he was for long ticks of the grandfather clock in the foyer and then followed her.

"Nice place," he said, clearing his throat then accepting the tea she offered.

"I liked it." Seline sat back, well aware of the contrast she made in her black leather against the floral sofa. She crossed her legs and swung her booted foot.

"You used the past tense."

"I did." She sipped the tea. "Because I'll have to leave now that I've been found."

"Because I've found you."

"Because you have no idea the can of worms you opened when you walked through that door."

She watched him grin. He didn't have clue one what he'd done. And she couldn't blame him. In fact, she gave him a lot of credit. She'd lived at the manor for over three years without being uncovered. Yet this one man had somehow found her in a little over a week.

She'd known sleeping with him wasn't a very good idea. Men like Ryder had egos as large as…well, as large as hers. They fed on challenges and she'd posed a challenge to him. Not just on the financial end, although she was sure that had stung him. No, rather they relished themselves in the role of love 'em and leave 'em bachelors and they didn't cotton to having their own behavior turned around on them.

She rested her elbow against the back cushion so she could look at him more fully. "I'd forgotten your background."

A chip in his armor.

"Marines, studying at Columbia even as you fought to make your way up the business ladder.

A ladder that once bore your family's name on a golden ring but that had collapsed under your grandfather's weight before you were born. Little-known associations with some shady characters."

Everything about him tensed.

"It seems I made a grave miscalculation."

"Seems that you did."

There was a sound outside on the grounds. Ryder heard it as well, but he appeared to be more interested in her start at it. Which meant she'd just revealed her own chip.

Casually putting her cup down, Seline stepped to the front window and looked out. A visiting gardener had just put down a wheelbarrow full of annuals he was about to plant around the front shrubs. She hadn't known she was rubbing her arms or that Ryder had joined her until he spoke.

"You're spooked."

Seline considered him long and hard. "You have no idea…."

7

RYDER TRIED to penetrate the tough exterior of the enigmatic woman before him.

She avoided his gaze and stepped around him. "If you'll excuse me a minute, I'd really like to get out of these clothes and wash up after my ride."

Ryder reached out and grasped her arm before he knew that's what he was going to do.

She stared at him. "Do you really think I'd try to bolt after you've somehow managed to find me?"

"I think exactly that."

"Fine," she said, smiling. "Then feel free to follow me."

Ryder wasn't sure what he was leaving himself open for, but staying behind in the living room waiting for her return wasn't even a remote option for him.

Jeeves was in the foyer as they passed. "Shall I arrange for dinner, ma'am?"

"You hungry?" she asked Ryder.

"No."

"Just leave a tray of sandwiches and finger foods, Jeeves. Then you can retire."

"Yes, ma'am."

Ryder got the impression that the two shared more than a mistress-butler relationship. It was something in the way Jeeves looked at Seline. But he couldn't figure out the connection. Friends? Did he help her with her cons? He didn't know. But he didn't think it was a good idea to underestimate the other man, nonetheless, despite how amused he'd been when Ryder had shown up at the door.

He watched Seline's leather-clad bottom lead the way up the winding staircase, then followed her down the hall to a room at the far end. She opened the door then turned toward him.

"Surely you don't plan to watch me change?" she asked, batting her eyes in a way that he might have bought nine days ago.

"That's exactly what I had planned."

She stared at him for a long moment, then walked inside the room. "Have it your way."

"That's exactly the way I intend to have it." Ryder closed the door after himself then looked around.

Various shades of white were everywhere,

with a throw pillow and chaise here and there in red velvet, probably placed so as not to completely blind the room's inhabitant.

Seline went to a closet and began to shimmy out of her black leather jeans. Ryder crossed his arms and openly enjoyed the view. She wore a pair of skimpy purple panties that hugged her rounded bottom to perfection. And those legs... He'd seen how long they were during their night together, but still the sheer length and curve of them threw him. Legs like that on a woman as beautiful as Seline Sanborn ought to be illegal.

He caught the ridiculous thought and grinned.

Seline reached inside the closet for a silky white robe then stepped into what he guessed was the master bath. She began to close the door.

"Oh no you don't." He caught the door before she could close it.

Finally he appeared to get a reaction from her other than cool control. "Knock it off, Blackwell. I'm not going to let you watch me take a shower." Then, just like that, the irritation was gone as she smiled. "Not without paying."

"Don't you think I've given enough already?"

She stepped aside. "Go ahead. Take a look around. No windows. Nowhere for me to go aside from back into this room."

Ryder examined the well-appointed bathroom with its steam shower and hot tub and was sorry that he didn't have an excuse to watch her. The thought of suds skimming her wet flesh was definitely a turn-on.

He looked at his Rolex as he stepped back into the bedroom. "You have ten minutes."

TEN MINUTES were more than enough for Seline to be well away from Ryder Blackwell.

She turned the lock on the door, switched on the shower, then moved the decorative screen away from the far wall and considered the secret passageway hidden in the ceramic tiles. Then she sighed and sat heavily down on a dressing-room chair, staring at the invisible entrance. Truth was, she didn't want to go.

She told herself it had to do with her need to find out how Ryder had uncovered her name and location, but she knew it was more than that. It went well beyond her reluctance to leave this house behind without a backward glance.

Simply put, Ryder Blackwell intrigued her in a way no man had been able to do in a long, long time.

She recalled Jeeves' knowing expression downstairs and suppressed a groan. It was just like her butler to invite Ryder inside—he kept telling her it was long past time she had a man in her life. She always told him that he was more man than she'd ever need, but the quietly homosexual Brit merely grinned at her and said that he didn't swing that way.

She stared at the secret doorway again, then looked over her shoulder at the door on the other side of which Ryder waited. She supposed it was enough for now to know that she could escape if she had to. While she always had at least three exit routes in any situation, she also had the added advantage of this being her home court. She knew every inch of the place up and down.

And if need be she could leave it faster than Ryder could use his considerable skills to bring her to orgasm.

So she moved the screen back into place along with the chair and took a quick shower, then exactly when Ryder knocked on the door to tell her that her ten minutes were up, she opened it and flashed him more than a dirty smile.

AN ALARM went off in Ryder's head as he stood looking at Seline in her slinky robe, the ends of her dark hair damp and leaving wet spots on the front…right where her breasts were. Her areolas were clearly outlined and her slightly protruding nipples made his mouth water with the desire take his fill of them.

"Happy?" she asked.

Happy wasn't the word for it. Certain parts of his body were downright ecstatic with her wanton display. Especially when his attention moved south to where her robe didn't quite close in the front, baring her cleanly shaven womanhood to his hungry gaze.

She leisurely pulled the robe more tightly closed, blocking his view, then moved toward the bed. "So, Ryder, you haven't told me yet whether you have been in contact with the authorities."

"No. I haven't told you." And he didn't plan on telling her, either. Although he figured she could guess that he hadn't.

So he'd wanted…no, needed to see her reaction when she realized he'd found her. He figured he could always call in the proper authorities if it came down to it.

Only as he watched her move around the intimate confines of her bedroom, it wasn't so much about what was down, but rather what was up. Namely his desire to show her exactly how much frustration she'd caused him over the past week and a half. How much he'd wanted to get even with her one moment, to just plain wanting her, period, the next.

He'd never felt anything quite similar before. The money Seline had swindled would have been a clear deal-breaker in any other context. But somehow he was currently having a problem connecting the crime to the criminal.

It could be the dispassionate nature of the act itself. She hadn't stolen from him because of revenge. Or because she was desperate. In fact, she hadn't stolen from *him* at all, but from Blackwell & Blackwell. And while it might seem that he and the company were one and the same, they weren't.

And he was just now coming to understand how very true that was.

What Seline had done was nothing more than a financial transaction. Not unlike what he might do to business competitors himself. Hold up a big contract here, pull strings to deny a bank loan or scare away investors there—what he did on a day-to-day basis could be argued to be along the same lines.

The difference lay in that what he did was viewed as business as usual. What she did was a prosecutable crime.

He blinked, just then realizing that she was

sitting on the bed applying lotion to her smooth skin. And he was so occupied with his thoughts he hadn't noticed.

Or rather his mind hadn't noticed. His body was fully aware that her nearly bare body was nearby.

He pulled a chair closer to the bed and sat down, stretching his feet to rest against the end of the bed, crossing his hands over his abdomen.

"So business must be good," Ryder commented, looking around the room, though time and time again his hungry gaze returned to her glistening skin, made softer still by the lotion she rhythmically applied to every inch.

"Can't complain. You?"

He shrugged. "I have a complaint or two, but nothing I can't handle."

Her hands slowed and she looked at him under her fringe of lashes. "Oh?"

"Mmm."

She finished with the lotion then lay back against the pillows, looking at him suggestively. Her right leg moved provocatively over the other, her slender foot rubbing the inside then the outside of the other calf. "Mind sharing exactly what you plan to do?"

"Yes, I do mind."

She tugged on the end of the belt holding the robe closed. "Too bad."

"Isn't it just?"

The belt untied and the robe gaped slightly open, revealing the flesh between her full breasts. "I think it's a pretty safe bet that the law isn't involved."

Ryder found it suddenly difficult to swallow. "Yet."

She tugged on the edge of the robe, causing the material over her right breast to fall away. He took in the taut puckered nipple. "Dependent on…" she led, her voice growing softer.

"Dependent on how this goes?"

"And what's 'this,' exactly?"

"The next few minutes."

He saw her tense slightly, but just as quickly she appeared to regain momentum as she orchestrated the baring of her other breast.

"Are you saying if I sleep with you, you'll leave?"

He blinked up into her eyes, which were inscrutable.

Seline abruptly sat up and pulled the robe closed. "Screw you, Blackwell." She strode toward the hallway door.

Ryder rose to his feet and caught her around the wrist, pulling her to him.

"Let me go."

"Not until I get what I came here to get."

"If that's sex—"

"It has nothing to do with sex."

Well, that wasn't entirely true. But at least it didn't in the way she thought it did.

"I came here for some answers."

"Right."

Ryder allowed his gaze to travel over her. He was certain that she probably knew at least a dozen ways to escape his grip. Yet she stayed where she was, perhaps allowing him to think he had the upper hand.

"Why did you sleep with me, Seline?"

"It seemed like a good idea at the time."

"Did it?"

"No, actually it didn't. But I wanted to anyway." She swung her long hair over her shoulder and glared at him. "As you probably already figured out, I'm a bit of a risk-taker."

"But sleeping with me put more at risk than I'm guessing you usually do."

She stared at him for a long moment as if trying to piece together the puzzle of his reasoning. "Are you thinking I slept with you because I felt more than desire?"

Ryder broke eye contact, damning himself even as he did so.

He cleared his throat then fought to maintain his gaze. "I'm saying that on a level you may currently be reluctant to acknowledge, you knew that if you slept with me you'd make your con personal. That I would come to find you."

"Yes, but trying and actually finding are two different things."

What might have been her next words fell silently between them.

Until now.

8

Until now.

Seline stared back at Ryder, inordinately aware of how heavily her heart beat against her ribcage. For a moment she'd forgotten that men like Ryder didn't come to be where they were because they allowed fundamental desires to get in the way of their goals. He hadn't come here for sex. He'd come for answers.

And the sheer thrill associated with finding an unfindable woman.

She wasn't aware of what changed between them in that one moment. But she did know that it had changed. She was back to the time she'd originally given up fighting her attraction to him and instead had given herself over to emotion.

Did he have any idea how he affected her? She searched his eyes even as the hand at her wrist began to caress instead of grip. No, she suspected he didn't.

However, she could see that he responded to whatever attraction existed between them as powerfully as she did.

"I thought you said sex had nothing to do with this," she murmured, even as her gaze moved to his mouth, longing for him to kiss her.

"It didn't."

"You used the past tense."

"That's because it no longer applies."

She met him when he bent to kiss her, her hands immediately going to his hair, her body arching against his. His groan filled her ears as she swirled her tongue around the inside of his mouth. He tasted of bourbon and desire. Like temptation personified.

Her robe disappeared first, followed quickly by his slacks and shirt and briefs. He nearly tossed her to the bed, where she bounced against the mattress as he bent over her. His hands claimed her breasts, his lips her mouth. She wrapped her legs around his waist, wanting and seeking. When he didn't immediately deliver, she rolled him over and straddled him, sitting upright, her sex in direct contact with his.

"Condom," he said.

She reached into the nightstand drawer and

pulled one out, but held it in her palm without opening it.

Ryder openly watched her, curiosity hiking one dark brow.

Seline moved her hips so that the long, hard length of his erection was sandwiched between her swollen labia. Ryder's pupils grew by degrees, nearly overtaking the electric blue of his eyes. She could tell it was taking all his willpower not to buck his hips so he could enter her without protection. She slid down the length of him again, pausing so that the tip rested against her tender bud. She was so hot for him a powerful shudder ran through her. Her juices covered him, lubricating the harmless bit of foreplay.

Rather than sheathing him with the latex, she dropped the condom to the top sheet then leaned over, putting her breasts in close proximity to his face. He took full advantage, curving his fingers around one of the sensitive globes then sucking her nipple against his tongue. Her reaction was such that she nearly couldn't concentrate on what she wanted to do. Nearly. She undid the white satin cord holding the wispy white canopy curtains back, then leaned to the right to get the other one there. Then she grasped his hands and lifted them high above his head, kissing him deeply.

"I'm the one who's supposed to be punishing you," he murmured, watching as she tied first one of his wrists to the bedpost, then the other.

"Who said I was punishing you?" she asked.

Even as she said the words, she knew there was a dark place within that demanded he acquiesce to her wishes. Allow her the control that his mere appearance at her estate had ripped from her.

Finally satisfied that he couldn't free himself without doing some damage, she wriggled her bottom back upright, considering his impressive male physique.

God, but the man was stunning. She flattened her palms against the well-defined muscles of his chest, then shifted them slowly over his collarbone and shoulders, then down toward his stomach. Springy light hair tickled her fingers as she worked her hands back up, bending to lave his flat male nipples with her tongue.

His erection throbbed between her legs. She tipped her hips forward, then back, then slid down his legs until her mouth was parallel with his distended flesh.

She watched with hooded eyes as he swallowed thickly. And the instant her mouth closed over the head of his arousal, he strained his neck and groaned.

Seline guessed it wasn't often that Ryder Blackwell gave up control. And while a part of her wondered why he was doing so now—after all, it would be all too easy for her to get up and leave him tethered to her bed while she made her escape—an even bigger part of her wanted to stick around and see why.

She grasped his thick width in her palm, moving her fingers down until the back of her knuckles met with his swollen sac. Holding him upright, she flicked her tongue over the straining flesh, tasting herself on him, tasting him as his own liquid beaded on the mushroom head. She moved her mouth down until she covered the hood then applied suction. His hips bucked against the mattress, forcing another inch inside her mouth even as he pulled at his restraints, the evidence of his coming climax making her hotter yet.

And she was nowhere near done.

Squeezing her fingers more tightly against his girth, she nudged her hand up, then down, mimicking the movements with her mouth…up and down…up and down…

With her free hand, she weighed his balls, not

about to leave them out. Ryder's deep groan told of his appreciation.

She sensed his impending orgasm and quickened her actions, then removed her mouth, watching as his semen exploded from him, his hips bucking violently against the mattress.

Seline then set about cleaning him all up.

RYDER HAD NEVER BEEN that big on receiving blow jobs. Quite frankly, he enjoyed being the one in command when it came to sex. But Seline's expert ministrations were giving him cause to rethink his entire take.

He tried to move his hands to cup her face and draw her up for a kiss, only to be reminded that he was bound to the heavy four-poster bed. As if the burning chafing of his wrists hadn't been enough.

It seemed that the woman lapping his penis with her tongue was introducing him to all kinds of firsts.

He watched as his semi-aroused flesh began to grow rock-hard again.

Seemingly satisfied, Seline lifted her head, sweeping her long dark hair to the other side of her face even as she straddled his hips again, giving him a clear view of her nude womanhood as she settled over him.

Dear Lord, the woman was determined to be the death of him.

"Untie me now?" he rasped.

She smiled and kissed him, the taste of both of them on her tongue. "Not just yet."

He watched as she finally tore open the foil packet with her teeth and sheathed him with the condom. Then she reached her fingers between her thighs and parted her swollen flesh. Ryder swallowed hard at the sight of the pink, tender pathway as she slowly slid down his engorged length.

For long moments he could do little more than lie there trying to gather his wits about him. His lungs were frozen, his every muscle tense. He tugged on his restraints again at the same time as she moved.

Ryder was mesmerized by the sight of her straddling him. Her face was an artist's rendering of bliss. Of a woman who not only wasn't afraid of sex, but knew how to thoroughly enjoy it. Her breasts heaved. Not as a result of her movements, but rather her quick, shallow breathing. Her skin glistened with moisture and that dark hair…that thick dark cloud framed her face as she slid back, then forth, her stomach muscles clenching as she did.

He longed to touch her. To caress her breasts. To clutch her hips. To roll her over so he could thrust into her as deep as he would go. The fact that he couldn't had an interesting effect on him. He felt on the verge of climax and frustrated by turns. He'd raise his hips to meet her and she'd move slightly away, only to slide back over him again, her sweet essence coating his member.

He heard her deep intake of breath and watched as every part of her seem to tremble. Her hair, her breasts, her stomach. He thrust his hips upward, going even deeper, and she moaned.

And he blasted right over the precipice with her.

The loud crash of broken glass sounded appropriate to him, so he didn't make much of it. Until he saw the shocked expression on Seline's face.

She rolled quickly away.

Ryder looked behind him at where the glass window had completely shattered. Something crashed to the floor in the room and he jerked as holes appeared in the opposite door and wall.

Bullet holes.

He opened his mouth to speak but Seline was quickly unbinding his hands.

"Follow me!" she shouted over the sounds of breakage around them.

She slid over the side of the bed to the floor

and he followed, gathering his clothes as he crab-walked toward into the bathroom. The bullet holes climbed the door as he passed, showering him with splinters.

"Haul ass, Blackwell!"

Where? Where could they possibly go inside the bathroom?

No windows. He remembered having checked the room out before she'd showered.

Still, the fact that someone was shooting at them didn't leave a lot of options. Was there only one shooter? Or was another making his way through the house even now?

He quickly dressed in his slacks and pulled on his shirt, watching in silence as Seline moved a chair and a changing screen, then pulled open a hidden door.

"Go!"

Ryder didn't need to be told twice. He had to stoop to fit into the short opening, but there was plenty of room to maneuver. Seline followed, pulling the door closed behind her and driving home a series of locks. It was pitch-black until she switched on a flashlight then passed him, leading the way through a maze of dark pathways, picking up small black bags along the way.

He couldn't hear the gunshots anymore, but

whether that was good or bad, he couldn't be sure. If there was no sound to mask their movements, could the gunman or men be listening for their progress?

Finally Seline pulled to a stop in front of him. She shut off the flashlight and he heard rustling. Then she opened up another door, revealing that she had dressed in black clothing she'd apparently found in one of the bags she'd collected.

"Here," she said, shoving a nickel-plated 9mm pistol at him.

Ryder blinked as she jumped the three feet down into what seemed to be the garage. She made a beeline straight for the Ducati he'd watched her ride up on earlier.

She was about to start it when her gaze snapped up to meet his. "Are you coming? Or would you prefer to wait around for them to catch up with you?"

Ryder stuffed the pistol into the back waist of his slacks then jumped. The tiled floor was cold under his bare feet as he quickly buttoned his shirt.

"Move back. I'm going to drive."

"Over my dead body."

Gunshots sounded on the other side of the garage door.

"What about Jeeves?" he asked, deciding not

to argue with her just then and climbing onto the seat behind her.

"He can take care of himself." She started the bike. "Besides, somebody has to stay behind to destroy the house."

"Destroy…"

The bike lurched at the same time she pushed a button, popping open a small opening in the garage door. A door they flew through.

Seline made a sharp left, angling them nearly parallel with the cement driveway, then leveled out and hit the gas, the powerful Italian engine growling beneath them as she zigzagged down the long drive, past two dark SUVs.

Ryder looked over his shoulder to find that one of the vehicles was turning around to give chase.

"Hold on," Seline said.

Then she veered off the main road, negotiating a path through a tangle of vegetation he half suspected had been placed there to give the motorcycle an advantage over, say, an SUV.

Jesus, he thought, tightening his grasp on her when the cycle went airborne just as the house behind him exploded, giving the sun a run for its money in the brightness department. Just what in the hell had he gotten himself into?

9

"YOU'RE HIT."

An hour later, Seline stopped at an out-of-the-way gas station in northern Illinois that still had old analog pumps and an old man manning the register, with nary an expensive bottle of water on display anywhere.

She looked down at where she'd absently tucked her right hand inside her leather jacket and drew it out. Blood coated her fingertips. "It's nothing," she said. "A flesh wound."

She'd been shot twice in her life, but that didn't automatically qualify her for expert status on gunshot wounds. However, she knew enough to understand that her continued mobility and endurance an hour after the hit meant that her wound wasn't too serious.

"Do you have your cell phone?" she asked Ryder.

"It's in my briefcase back at your place."

She fished around in the backpack tied to the bike and tossed a cell his way. "Make arrangements to get yourself back to New York. I'm going to clean up."

Without sparing him another glance, she walked to the station office, got the restroom key that was attached to what seemed like the trunk of an oak tree, then let herself into the ancient bathroom off to the side. Not bothering to lock the door, she shrugged out of her jacket, careful not to jostle her right shoulder too much, and considered the damage in the scratched mirror.

Damn.

She poked around. As she'd suspected, it was only a minor wound. But it had put a hole through her shoulder and might have nicked her clavicle in the process. She took off her black tank top, soaked it with hot water, then squeezed it out over the wound, cringing with pain as she cleaned the blood from her skin so she could get a better look. A wave of dizziness hit her and she leaned against the chipped porcelain sink for support.

"Who in the hell *are* you?"

She didn't bother opening her eyes. She'd heard Ryder enter the unlocked room. "Someone you should never have gotten involved with."

"I knew that the first night," he said.

She stared at him.

"But that doesn't change the fact that I chose to get involved anyway." He took the tank top from her and wrung it out. "Turn around."

She did as requested, clenching her teeth against the dizziness that refused to go away, barely aware that she was naked from the waist up.

"Gunfights a normal part of the job for you?" he asked quietly, gingerly patting her shoulder with the tank top then rinsing the fabric out again.

"Not normally."

"But you have been involved in them before."

It was more of a statement than a question so she didn't acknowledge it.

"You're right," he said after long minutes. "The bullet appears to have traveled clean through."

"Nice shoes," she said, noticing that he wore an old pair of work boots.

"Thanks. I gave the old geezer a ten spot for them."

"His?"

"I hope not. His feet were smaller than a ten-year-old girl's. He got them out of the garage."

Seline moved to get iodine and gauze from the bag she'd brought in with her.

"Let me. While it doesn't appear that you've lost a lot of blood, you're pale as a communion wafer."

She cocked a brow at his description.

Within minutes he'd neatly dressed her wound then handed her a white tank top that was packed with the kit.

"Not bad," she said, examining his handiwork before carefully putting the top on. "Do this often?"

"Once or twice in the military."

"Ah, yes. The marines. Bosnia."

He grimaced as he threw away the wrappings.

"No, not there." She took out a plastic bag. "We should leave as little as possible behind in case they come this way."

"*They* being?"

She didn't answer, just stuffed her bloodied tank top and the wrappings into the bag, then tied it up, cleaning the sink and the floor around her feet with ammonia. Even if Luminol picked up a blood trace, the evidence would be unusable so long as she covered it all.

"Did you make the call?" she asked, leading the way from the bathroom with both bags in tow. She gave the station attendant the tree trunk back, paid for the gas she'd filled the bike with, then walked toward the waiting Ducati.

"No."

She swiveled toward him. "Look, Ryder, you

being with me isn't a good idea. One target is harder to follow than two."

She secured both bags to the bike.

"Go back to the city. Surround yourself with security. Lay low until everything blows over." She mounted the Ducati. "It's me they want, not you."

He grasped her right arm, causing her to wince in pain. "Who in the hell are *they*, Seline?"

"It doesn't matter. What does is that your innocent game of cat and mouse led them straight to my doorstep." She caught his wince and briefly bit her bottom lip. "Go home, Ryder."

"And if I refuse?"

She stared at him. "Why would you refuse? This is my problem, not yours."

"Yes, but if it's true what you said, that I'm the one who led the gunmen to you, then I'm in this as far as it goes."

"Not if you leave now."

He looked around. "Where would you have me go?"

She fished the cell from his front pocket, flicked it open, then shoved it in his direction. "With your resources, you should be able to get a 'copter here to pick you up in a matter of minutes."

"I'll do that on one condition. That you come with me."

"Not an option." She started the bike.

He climbed on the back.

"What in the hell are you doing, Blackwell?"

"Going with you."

She revved the engine several times but didn't move. "Get off or I'll force you off."

"Goddamn it, Seline. Either you come with me or I go with you. One or the other. You choose. But I'll be damned if I'm just going to let you ride off into the sunset."

She squinted to the west, finding that, indeed, the sun was setting in a fiery glow over the horizon.

"Red sky at night, thief's delight. Red sky in the morning, thief take warning."

She recalled the twist on the old sailor saying that her father had repeated a few times.

But he'd had no way of knowing that she would be right where she was in that moment, with a stubborn, handsome male on the back of her bike refusing to get off.

She gunned the engine, half hoping he'd fall off the back. But he'd anticipated her move and barely blinked at her in the rearview mirror.

DOWNTOWN Chicago was the next stop. Even though only an hour and a half had passed since the first bullet had shattered Seline's bedroom window, Ryder felt as if it could have been a month and a half. He climbed from the bike only after Seline had cut the engine and removed the key, looking around at the packed parking lot of a bar named Jazzy's. Did Seline crave a stiff brew?

He noticed she was a little slow getting off the cycle.

"Are you okay?" he asked, steadying her.

"I'm fine." She gathered various items from the bike, including the garbage bag from the gas station, and headed in the opposite direction from the bar entrance. He followed.

"You'll want to go the other way," she said.

He looked over his shoulder.

"You'll find at least three hotels to check into until you can make arrangements to return to New York."

"And you?"

She stared at him as she continued walking. "We already discussed this."

"Yes, we did. And I made my stand clear."

No matter how bizarre the past hour and a half had been when compared to his normal life, he wasn't a man who cut and run at the first sign of trouble. While he'd had no way of knowing how heavy the baggage Seline Sanborn carried was, he'd known there would be some. She'd stolen a cool three-quarters of a million from his company. That alone indicated complications.

Of course, he hadn't exactly expected to sleep with her again, either. If asked to guess how he'd saw things going down when she'd returned to her estate earlier, he'd have said would run more along the lines of, "Hello, I found you," and a call to the proper authorities to enjoy watching her be arrested for the crime. After he got his money back.

How far away that all seemed now.

More specifically, hot sex, a gunshot wound, a manic motorcycle escape and a massive explosion ago.

Items of that nature had a way of putting a different spin on things.

Survival.

"One doesn't fight wars," his father had once quoted to him. "One survives them."

He'd shared the wisdom the night Ryder had told him he'd signed up for a stint in the marines.

The elder Blackwell was as pacifist as they came and he hadn't been pleased with his son's decision to go into the military. But Ryder's grades hadn't been high enough to earn him a scholarship to Columbia, his school of choice, and since his father couldn't afford the tuition and he wasn't about to take on a ton of student loan debt, the military and the GI bill emerged a solid option.

Of course, neither he nor his father could have anticipated Somalia or Bosnia or Kosovo.

He'd seen far more action than he'd antici-pated. And lost two close buddies as a result.

He wasn't about to leave a man behind. Even if this man was a woman. Who had stolen from him.

"I can have both of us in a safe house within a hour," he said to her back now.

She laughed.

He rounded her, forcing her to stop and consider him. "I'm serious, Seline."

He noticed a flash of something in her eyes. Surprise? Gratitude? Whichever it was, the expres-sion that followed soon after told him she was going to turn him down flat. "Thanks, but no thanks."

"Your activities at Blackwell & Blackwell need never be mentioned."

"And just how would you explain what happened at my house?"

"The ultimate in home invasions? Mistaken identity?"

She smiled then circled him to continue walking. "Not going to happen. First," she said, holding up a finger, "you'll have to involve the authorities." She raised a second finger. "Second, whichever channels you used to locate me have already led them to me. How long do you think it'll take for them to find me again? Third…"

He walked at her side. "Third?"

She looked at the sidewalk ahead of her. "Third, while I appreciate your show of whatever outdated act of chivalry you think you're performing, I prefer to work alone."

And with that, Ryder suspected Seline had put her finger on exactly the reason why he couldn't, wouldn't walk away. Simply because he recognized himself in her. Not in her actions or her being a moving target for something bigger than he could currently wrap his mind around. But the fact that they were both loners, used to depending on themselves and themselves only in order to get something done.

He'd heard of opposites attracting. But loners? Was it possible that the recognition alone was enough to draw him to a woman he'd known he had no business getting involved with even before getting shot at? To feel a connection to her that transcended all common sense and rationale and compelled him to do something so outside his normal M.O. as to be almost ridiculous?

"Are you still here?"

He grinned at her. "Get used to it. Because I don't plan on going anywhere anytime soon."

10

HER GODMOTHER had once claimed that Seline was a stupid-man magnet. Put her in the middle of a street and every stupid man within a five-block radius would find his way to her.

And despite all prior evidence to the contrary, it appeared Ryder Blackwell was as dumb as a bag of rocks.

She shook her head as she walked, turning off the main drag, going up two blocks, hanging a right, another left, then navigating an overgrown alleyway that ran between businesses and houses until she came to a one-car garage that was in dire need of good lighting and a paint job. Using a key she found under a loose board to the right of the door, she let herself in, grimacing when Ryder followed. Her shoulder ached like nobody's business and she could do with a massive infusion of sugary liquids and sleep. The last thing she needed was a curious greenhorn with illusions of being her knight in shining armor hanging around.

Especially if she was the one who was going to be doing the rescuing.

Swiping cobwebs out of the way, she walked around to the front of an old 1969 Chevy SS Camaro Z28 that was more a bondo special than the navy blue with white stripes it originally had been. She unplugged the battery charger, took off the contact claws and reattached the engine cables before closing the hood.

"Watch it."

Seline had known exactly where Ryder was—standing off to the side staring at the powerful engine—before she'd closed the hood.

"Yours?" he asked as she climbed between the wheel.

"In a manner of speaking."

He climbed in the passenger seat. "Like Carol Lambert's identity?"

She turned the key in the ignition, the roar of the engine making conversation impossible. Even if she'd been interested in offering it.

She gunned the engine a couple of times, then climbed out and counted four rusted old coffee cans to the right and three down on the dusty shelves. Pulling a can down, she fished through the three plastic bags of IDs there, found the one she wanted, emptied out the contents then put her current IDs inside, closed the can and put it back on the shelf with the other.

"Jesus, you have this down to a science, don't you?" Ryder said quietly, looking over her shoulder.

"Comes with the territory."

She started to open the garage door, wincing at the strain it put on her shoulder, then gladly stepped aside when he offered to do it for her. She backed out into the lane, and he began to close the door again.

Without a moment of hesitation, she gunned the engine and roared down the alley, leaving Ryder behind.

HE SHOULD HAVE seen that one coming.

Ryder watched the cloud of dust rise up to envelop the one glowing streetlight in the alley and shook his head.

Then he ran full out into the yard between the garage he'd just closed and the next, the over-grown vegetation slightly impeding his progress as he moved. He jumped over two low fences and emerged onto the street just as Seline turned the corner. She squealed to a stop mere millimeters away from where he stood, blocking the road that was down to one lane given the cars parked at both curbs.

She revved the engine and lurched forward, the front bumper nudging his knees.

Ryder met her gaze through the window even as he fought to catch his breath.

He'd have been in sorry shape had she chosen to turn the other way. No amount of running would have allowed him to catch up with her.

But thankfully his luck was good and she had the choice of running him over, letting him in or backing up.

The third option was taken away from her when another car pulled up behind her and the driver lay on the horn.

"Christ. Get in, already," she said.

He climbed into the car. His head snapped back when she hit the gas.

"That wasn't very nice."

"I was trying to do you a favor."

"Yeah, well, don't do it again." He pulled some sort of vegetation from inside the hem of his pants. "I probably ran through poison ivy."

He looked over to find her grinning.

"That's not even remotely funny."

"Humor is relative."

"You find my running after you amusing?"

"I find the thought of you with poison ivy slightly funny, yes."

"Yeah, well, just so you know, you're the one who's going to have to apply the calamine lotion."

And just like that Ryder found himself sharing a smile with Seline Sanborn that had nothing to do with their situation or her stealing from him or trying to leave him behind, and everything to do with the connection he could sense forming between them.

It was his reference to the future.

He guessed it wasn't often that Seline could look beyond the next few hours, much less look forward to them in the company of someone other than her butler.

Of course, he wouldn't have dared crack such a joke in the company of any of the women he'd dated over the past couple of years. Not that he'd classify what was happening as a date by any stretch. But…

Before long they were on the highway heading west. A half hour into the trip, Ryder found his gaze was still on her. He found it incredible that even without makeup and with much of the color drained from her face, she had to be the most fascinatingly beautiful woman he'd ever met.

His gaze dropped to her posture; she sat stiffly.

He lightly touched her shoulder and she winced. He pulled back the jacket to find her T-shirt showing blood.

"You're bleeding again."

"I'll live."

"I'm glad you're confident."

She gave him a long look.

"I think we're safe for the time being. Pull over and let's change the dressing and get you some fluids."

Surprisingly, she did as he requested.

After getting something to eat, several bottles of mineral water and a cooler with ice in which to put them, they returned to the car, both of them reaching for the driver's side door handle at the same time.

Ryder won.

"Let me take the next shift," he said. "Do you have a blanket or something in the trunk?"

"There might be something."

She must have been feeling worse than she was letting on because she didn't fight him when he took the keys from her hand. He moved to the trunk, pulled out a plastic-encased pillow and blanket then opened the driver's door, sprang the seat release and placed both items in the back seat.

"Get in."

She did as asked, stretching out as best as she could with the pillow behind her head. Ryder unfolded the blanket and placed it over her legs, feeling an odd nurturing sensation.

When was the last time he'd had to take care of anyone? Never, he realized.

"How do I know you won't take me back to New York?" she asked, wincing even as her eyes drooped closed.

"Because you're going to tell me where to go. Outside hell, that is."

She managed a small smile. "Stay on 66 heading west."

"Until?"

"Until I tell you not to."

He had begun to put the driver's seat upright when she grasped his hand.

Ryder paused. Her skin felt cold against his as he looked into her eyes.

"Ryder, I…"

He didn't help her out. Merely waited to hear what she had to say.

"Thanks."

It was more than her hesitation that told him that she wasn't used to thanking anyone, and what was usually a simple sentiment touched him.

"Don't mention it."

He righted the seat then climbed into the car. If her words and the fact that she was allowing him to take the lead had him feeling a bit cocky, he wasn't worrying about it.

He found the highway on-ramp and set out in the direction she'd indicated, trying to keep from looking at her sleeping face in the rearview mirror more than ten times a minute.

SELINE woke up with the sun across her face, her shoulder throbbing and her head feeling as if it was the size of a watermelon. The first thing she realized was that the car wasn't moving. The second was that Ryder was nowhere to be found.

She quickly moved to a sitting position and looked around. Arkansas. It had to be. And they were stopped at a rest area. She turned her watch around on her wrist. After noon.

Had she really slept for over fourteen hours in the back of a moving car? And had Ryder really driven all that way without stopping to sleep?

"Good, you're up."

Ryder held a cup of vending-machine coffee out to her. She took a deep pull then grimaced. "Like a little coffee with your sugar and cream?"

"That's not mine, it's yours. I figured you could use the sugar." He held up another cup. "Mine."

She moved to press the seat release.

"Whoa, where are you going?"

"Bathroom would be nice."

"Oh." He opened the door and held the seat for her, helping her climb out.

Seline gingerly stretched each of her muscles.

"How do you feel?"

"Like shit warmed over."

He chuckled. "You this cheerful every morning?"

"Yep." She started in the direction of the bathrooms.

"You need any help?"

"That's not where I was shot."

"I meant with redressing your wound."

She turned back, took the supply bag from him, then turned back again. "Thanks."

"Don't mention it."

"I won't again."

She threw a smile over her good shoulder to find him shaking his handsome head.

And it was handsome, wasn't it? Even sleep-deprived, with a good deal of stubble on his jaw and his hair wind-tousled, Ryder Blackwell looked almost more attractive to her now than he had before. He'd rolled up his sleeves past his elbows and had left the tails of his shirt out, his soiled slacks looking absurdly fitting against the oily work boots.

She imagined him in a pair of tight-fitting jeans and a T-shirt and found her mouth watering.

Stop it, Seline. At the first opportunity you've got to find a way to dump him.

First off, she'd been so out of it last night, she had no idea if he'd been in contact with anyone. If so, the men on her tail might be close to catching up with her even as she peed.

If he hadn't called anyone...

She swallowed hard, ranking that possibility up there with being just as dangerous as the gunmen. Men like Ryder Blackwell didn't have a selfless bone in their bodies. Oh, yeah, they were good in bed, so long as you could stand them, and they cleaned up well, but they would drop a dollar into a blind man's cup a hundred times without ever really noticing the person holding the cup was blind.

What Ryder was experiencing right now had everything to do with adrenaline and nothing to do with common sense. And as soon as he woke up from his bout of temporary insanity, he'd head straight back to his cozy, insulated life in New York and leave her high and dry.

It would be safer for her in the long run to just speed the process up for him.

The key lay in exactly how and when to do it....

11

"So TELL me," Ryder said from the passenger's seat. "How much money did you take that would warrant someone wanting you dead?"

Seline had driven over the Texas state line into New Mexico and heat rose in waves from the barren landscape around them, the impending dusk doing little to lower the high temperatures. The air circulating through the open windows helped dry the sweat coating her face, but didn't stop rivulets rolling between her breasts and down her back.

It was hotter than Hades and Ryder wanted to talk.

"Aren't you tired?"

She could feel his gaze on her and knew he was probably grinning. "No."

The loud hum of the engine would have kept most from attempting conversation. But not Ryder. Not that she could blame him. If their roles were reversed, she'd be looking for a little info herself.

"If they had wanted me dead, I would be dead."

She looked to find his right brow raised, waiting for her to give him more. She didn't.

"Money?"

"You could say that's part of it." She lifted her good arm and wiped her T-shirt sleeve against her forehead.

"The rest?"

"You always ask so many questions?"

They'd stopped awhile back for dinner at an out-of-the-way greasy spoon. He'd tried to pump her for info then, as well, but she'd quickly eaten her meatloaf and left as soon as she was done, forcing him to leave half his uneaten food behind.

"Is there anything else you'd suggest we do?"

Seline gave him a long look. The open invitation on his face was almost laughable. Almost. If only a part of her didn't respond in kind. A longing that started deep in her stomach and spread quickly north and south, sparking awareness that while personally she didn't know this man all that well…in bed, oh, in bed she knew too much.

He returned his attention to the road and

leaned his elbow on the door. "So you think I led these guys to you."

A statement of fact rather than a question. "I know you did."

"Funny, because I know I didn't."

"Come on, Ryder, you probably had a team of people looking for me. People who have contacts beyond you."

He shook his head. "In the beginning, yes I did. But they couldn't draw a bead on you."

She waited.

"It was an independent low-rent P.I. out of Brooklyn who found you. And only she and I were privy to the information."

"Then someone was following you."

"On the off chance that I'd happen to pay you a visit?"

"They're very determined."

"And I was very determined that I wouldn't be followed."

"Perhaps the Brooklyn P.I. was persuaded to share the info."

"Possible, but not probable. The high-end agencies I originally hired couldn't find you. What were the chances that she would?"

"Good point." She let her foot up slightly on the gas when she realized she was speeding. Not a good idea to get pulled over right now. "Which leads us back to your being followed."

"Did you see an unfamiliar car in your driveway?"

No, she hadn't. A car would have triggered suspicion before she'd entered the house.

"I drove a rental from O'Hare, pegged your estate, then parked at the edge of the driveway of one of your neighbors and put the hood up. Then I walked to your place."

"Quite a hike."

"Yeah, but worth it."

She remembered walking in to see him waiting for her. Recalled the moment of pleasure combined with dread. Pleasure that she could stop fantasizing about him. Dread that if he could find her, so could the others.

"You know, sleeping with me again probably wasn't a good idea," he said. "Once, a guy can overlook. Twice and he might begin to imagine a relationship."

Seline laughed. Not a surface giggle, but a gut-deep guffaw that left her coughing and shoulder throbbing.

Ryder's grin told her he liked her response.

"What, do you think only women can be romantics?"

She stared at him, the laughter filling her chest and staying. "There's nothing romantic about the sex we had, Ryder."

"Considering the sex, a guy could be persuaded differently."

"Ah, I see. Along the lines of, 'the way to a man's heart is through his stomach.'"

"Something like that."

"I might buy that if I didn't know more about you."

He moved so that he was partially facing her. "And just what do you think you know about me?"

"First," she said, holding up a finger. "You're a serial dater."

"Not unlike yourself."

"I don't date. I indulge in a series of one-night stands."

"The difference being?"

"Point granted." She raised another finger. "Second, you're so focused on your career that women and marriage rate low on your list of priorities, much less romance."

"Again, like you."

She narrowed her eyes. "And what do you think you know about me?"

He shrugged. "I didn't say I knew anything.

But you pointing out what you think you know about me is allowing me a bit of insight into you."

"Pop psychology."

"Perhaps. But true nonetheless, I'm guessing. I don't think your choice of careers is exactly conducive to much of a personal life outside your job. Which makes the finger you point at me accusing me of being a workaholic my number one, and the other fingers in your hand are also pointing back at you."

She looked to find that her hand was positioned in the way he'd outlined. She gripped the steering wheel.

"Third," she said, forgoing any more hand gestures on the grounds that they might incriminate her. "I don't think there's a woman out there that can live up to your high expectations."

Seline concentrated on the road, passing a large RV that was traveling five miles under the speed limit. After she'd moved back into the right lane she looked at Ryder to find him thoughtfully silent. "What, no crack about how I'm the same?"

"Did you just call me a snob?"

"Maybe."

Rather than taking offense, he appeared to be giving the possibility some consideration.

She wasn't used to that. And couldn't say

whether she would have given anything he said the same weight.

"My father says the same thing," he said quietly.

Father. Instantly Seline imagined a man twenty years or so Ryder's senior, essentially an older version of him with graying hair and that one cheek dimple that he used often when he smiled.

"He doesn't say I'm a snob so much as he's afraid I'm too choosy." He looked out the window. "He mentions grandchildren a lot."

"Being an only child must have its drawbacks."

"I didn't say I was an only child."

She stared at him.

"Oh." He ran his fingers through his thick dark hair. "Pre-con research. What do they call that, anyway? Pre-con recon?"

"Funny."

"Yeah, well, I'm not very amused right now."

And for some reason Seline couldn't pinpoint, it bothered her that he was bothered.

"I have two older brothers," she found herself offering. "We were all raised by our father."

She had his attention and he no longer looked bothered. Which was a good thing in her book. No matter what it might have cost her.

"Your mother?"

"My mother left the three of us on our father's doorstep when I was four and took off for parts unknown. Yours?"

He seemed surprised by her answer. "She was married to my father for twenty-five years before dying of breast cancer fifteen years ago."

"I'm sorry."

"Thanks."

The car fell silent for a stretch. A stretch that Seline used to reflect on her brothers and father who she hadn't seen in years and missed terribly.

"So where did you pick up your trade?" Ryder asked.

Seline shifted in her seat, regretting the instant she did because it made her more aware of her sweaty state.

What did she tell him? That her father had been one of the more successful conmen in New York City when she was growing up? That when she was twelve the law had finally caught up with him and he'd spent the next eight years at Riker's? That where she'd grown up gangsters and con artists and criminals and prison time were accepted aspects of life? That she'd pulled her first con when she was thirteen with her brother, netting her a cool grand? That despite her father trying to keep her from the life, she had enjoyed the rush of pulling a con too much to go back?

That her choices had ultimately demanded a price higher than she could have ever imagined? A price she was still paying and always would?

Seline didn't know what to share, so she shared nothing.

"Touchy subject?" he asked.

"Complicated." Too complicated to explain to a guy she'd had sex and little more with. Twice. "How about you? I mean, I understand that Blackwell used to be a big name about town before you were born, but what made you want to get it all back? To work toward the goal at the expense of all else?"

"At the expense of what?"

"I don't know. A wife. Kids. Normal family stuff."

"I consider my life normal."

She smiled. "I guess it all depends on your definition of normal then, doesn't it?"

He got her point and smiled back.

"Maybe you're right. Maybe we are more alike than either of us knows," she said. "I mean, it's not beyond the realm for you to pull some under-handed stunts to get a competitor to sell or to force them out of business or play rough with the union to get them to take fewer benefits or lower pay."

"The difference is that what I do is legal."

"That's because suits like you make the laws."

"Are you trying to say that what you do is legit?"

"What I'm trying to say is that I've never conned anyone who couldn't afford it. That I've never personally hurt anyone. I bet you can't say the same."

He looked out the window again. "But at the end of the day I don't get shot at."

Seline winced.

So Ryder gave as good as he got out of bed as well as in it. She could respect that.

"So do you plan to tell me where we're going?"

Seline had been so distracted by their conversation that she'd forgotten that she had planned to dump him long before now. As it stood, she was only three, four hours, max, away from her destination.

When was the last time she'd been distracted to such a degree? She couldn't recall. And it both baffled and intrigued her that Ryder had been the one to do it.

"You'll see," she said, giving herself over to the fact that she didn't want to dump him. Not just yet. She was interested in knowing what made the man tick. What made him track her down then go on the lam with her when it would have been smarter and easier for him to return to his regularly scheduled life.

And if some small part of her was actually beginning to like him, well, she wasn't going to admit it to herself much less to him.

12

AT AROUND 1:00 A.M. just outside Albuquerque, New Mexico, Seline pulled the car to the side of a long, empty road, slid her seat back and settled in for the night. Ryder did the same. And despite thinking he wouldn't be getting much sleep knowing Seline was within touching distance, he dropped off and didn't awaken again until after seven the next morning. He got a chance to see to business, and wash his face with bottled water before Seline was ready to go again.

Ryder had flown into Albuquerque in the past, but he couldn't remember seeing much of the area, probably because he'd been busy in the limo that had taken him from the airport to the hotel and to various meeting places, either on his laptop or on his cell following up on other business matters even as he'd traveled to one. But now that he was without limo, laptop and cell, he had nothing better to do than take in the distinct landscape around him.

That wasn't entirely true. He'd prefer to talk to Seline some more, but she'd fallen silent and had refused to be drawn in further, answering his questions with a simple yes, no or maybe if she answered at all.

That was fine. While there weren't many people he could share silence with without being uncomfortable or wanting to fill the void, Seline was proving to be one of them.

Maybe because when they talked, she gave him something to think about during those silences.

"Beautiful, isn't it?" Seline said as if half to herself.

Ryder looked at her. "Yes it is."

"Have you been out—" She caught the way he was looking at her and stopped. "Oh."

Ryder smiled to himself and looked back out the window.

Instead of taking the route into Albuquerque as he'd expected her to, she veered north toward Santa Fe, an area he definitely had never visited. He watched as the landscape gave way to smaller haciendas with tiny yards bursting with flowers. She exited the highway and drove for another half hour before finally pulling up in front of a guardhouse. Ryder looked behind the gate at the houses there, half expecting to find another estate the size of the one she'd had in Wisconsin.

"Hi, Gerry," she said to the guard. "I have a guest visiting."

"Name?"

"John Black."

"Very good, Miss Smith."

The gate lifted and they were allowed entrance into what looked like a modest subdivision. The houses were newer, but they were small, with plenty of privacy and set back from the street.

"Smith?" he asked.

"Yes. Sally Smyth, with a *Y*. Oh, and in case you should have opportunity, you don't want to get too friendly with the neighbors. You're more than likely to find yourself staring into the double barrel of a shotgun."

"If it's all the same to you, I think I've had enough of being on that side of a gun to last a lifetime."

"That's how the residents here feel. Some of them were abused wives, some parents of molested children where the spouse was the offender, others are crime victims who couldn't find a sense of safety anywhere else. A lot of them had no choice but to move here from all across the country."

"And you fit in where?"

Seline looked at him, her face fresh and open and nonjudgmental. "I play a small role in helping them achieve that safety and secure them jobs they can do from home." She gestured toward what appeared to be a community center. "We have our own elementary school, health and child care clinics and a staff of no fewer than fifty armed security guards."

Ryder couldn't take his eyes from her. "Sounds like a self-contained city."

She smiled faintly. "Something like that. There are nearly seven hundred and fifty residents, many in apartment complexes a little farther up the road. And we have a waiting list of at least a thousand."

He raised his brows at that. "I'm surprised you're telling me this."

"Me, too." She took a deep breath as she negotiated narrow streets that were empty of cars but full of kids. "But I figure if you ever change your mind and want to have me arrested, this may make it a little more difficult for you." She looked at him. "And how do *you* give back to the community, Mr. Blackwell?"

Now that was a question he hadn't been expecting, mainly because he was still trying to digest what she'd just told him.

Here she was, a con artist who attracted

gunfire and she had a hand in funding a safe haven for others. The contrast was stunning.

He said quietly, "The company makes its share of charitable contributions."

"I'm sure. But I'm not asking about the company. I'm asking about you. And don't try to make them sound like one and the same, because I'm not buying it. Companies like yours make the donations for PR and tax-write-off purposes."

"What would you have me do?"

Seline shrugged as she stopped the car so a boy of about five could get a ball that had bounced into the street. The kid's mother followed him to usher him out of the way, her wary gaze securely on Ryder.

"You could volunteer as a big brother. You used to play varsity basketball, how about coaching at a community center?"

He'd half expected her to say something along the lines of "why not create your own mini-city?" Instead, her suggestions were on a much smaller scale. And more hands-on.

"Hi, Jan," she said to the woman who was still looking at Ryder from where she now stood on the curb. "How's Jason coming along?"

"Better. He's sleeping through the nights now. Thanks for asking, Sally."

They spoke for a couple of more moments then Seline continued on down the road.

"Do you know everyone here?"

"Not everyone. My job," she said, giving him a loaded glance, "doesn't allow me to spend the time here that I'd like. But since I bought into the place six years ago, there's been an in-residence panel—the majority of whom came here like most everyone else—that oversees everything."

The con artist with the heart of gold.

Ryder rubbed his chin, just then realizing that he probably looked like a homeless guy. No wonder the mother had looked at him suspiciously, no matter that he was with Seline...or Sally...or Carol...

"Is Seline your real name?"

She merely smiled at him.

"This is it."

She turned into a long drive meandering back from the road over a large plot of land. The house was a one-story adobe house with a three-arch porch from which hung planters of vivid flowers. Large terra-cotta vases stood on either side of the door. The place looked airy and comfortable and, considering the size of her sprawling Wisconsin estate, very small.

A fiftyish woman who could have been of

Mexican or Native American heritage opened the door and stood wiping her hands on an apron. Seline parked the hot, dusty Camaro and climbed out and Ryder followed suit, the sudden stillness a bit of a shock to his road-weary body. He eyed the climbing sun. He'd had a long day before flying to Chicago and driving the rental to her Wisconsin estate, in addition to the two-day road trip they'd just taken. And it was a good long shower and sleep that he craved now.... He watched the gentle sway of Seline's bottom in her black jeans. Among other things.

Ryder closed the passenger door and followed her up to the porch.

"*Hola,* Señora Sally."

"*Hola,* Gurtza," Seline said, giving the other woman a quick, hard hug.

"I came the moment you call. I'm almost done readying the place now."

"Thank you, Gurtza. Whatever isn't done can wait. Why don't you go home now—I'll stop by in awhile."

"Very well, Señora Sally."

The older woman took off her apron and Seline accepted it with a smile, watching as she walked to a pickup truck and pulled from the drive. Within moments there was nothing but the sound of crickets and a nearby water fountain fashioned from terra-cotta vases in a small courtyard he could see through the open door. He and Seline were completely alone.

"Come on. I'll show you to the guest bedroom," she said, leading the way inside.

Ryder took in the sparsely but tastefully decorated living and dining areas as he passed. Ceiling fans whirled, and patio doors were opened to the courtyard that seemed to be in the center of the house, the point around which the entire house revolved like a wheel. He didn't feel air conditioning but it was comfortably cool inside.

"Guest room?" he asked as she stopped outside a door.

"I figured you'd want to get a shower. And since I do, too, this is the most obvious solution."

They'd stopped at a department store yesterday and he'd picked up a few items of clothing and shaving gear, feeling awkward that she had to pay for them even though it was likely with money she'd stolen from him and his company.

"Another option would be to shower together."

Seline smiled at him and then folded the apron over her arm. "I hope you're happy with your accommodations, Mr. Blackwell."

Ryder leaned against the wall and crossed his

arms, watching as she walked away from him. Every time he thought he had the provocative woman pegged, she'd do something completely unexpected.

While he couldn't be entirely certain, he thought he detected a New York City accent from time to time. Especially when she was getting heated up on a topic, like when they'd discussed the possibility of his being to blame for her un-invited, gun-toting guests back in Wisconsin. But how did a New York girl end up not just with a place in New Mexico, but the whole secure compound they were in? He considered that she could have gotten involved in the community as a result of her own need to hide from time to time, but that somehow didn't fit. While her job required that she disappear every now and again, he figured that there were at least a thousand different ways she could do that, with a fraction of the cash she'd obviously invested here. A thousand cars parked in garages across the country each with their own coffee cans of iden-tifications she could rely on to get her to her next destination.

Which made him even more curious about her. Had she been an abused wife? A violent crime victim?

While none of those titles seemed to fit Seline, neither had he imagined the street racer he'd first spotted in Manhattan, and slept with as Carol Lambert, was a thief about to con his company out of nearly a million dollars.

She'd long since disappeared down the circular hall. Ryder shook his head, pushed from the wall, then went into the guest room to get that shower that would, he hoped, help him think clearly now that the immediate danger of their situation was past.

TWO HOURS later, Seline stepped out of the shower in the master bedroom. After drying herself and attending to her wound, she left her damp hair hanging free over a nightshirt that brushed the tops of her thighs and plain white cotton underpants, and moved around the kitchen eating a light meal and drinking iced tea that Gurtza had left brewing in a jar in the New Mexican sun.

She then sat down at the table and picked up her cell phone, taping a pen against the pad she'd gotten from out of a drawer, the laptop at her elbow switched on, the browser pointed to three different nationwide crime-tracking Web sites and the Wisconsin newspaper closest to her estate.

Correction: former estate.

"Seline." Jeeves answered her call on the first ring.

She'd called him on the road, asking after his wellness and the status of the estate. The areas of the house she had needed "cleaned" were gone, fireproofing having protected her cars and leaving about seventy-five percent of the residence still intact...and bringing a hundred-and-ten percent interest from the local law-enforcement community that had managed to chase one of the SUVs toward Illinois, where they'd lost it.

"What's going on?" she asked him now.

"About the same as the last time we spoke."

She'd suspected as much. While Jeeves was her point man in Wisconsin, he wasn't plugged into New York, which was just the way she wanted it. She liked keeping the various aspects of her life compartmentalized. Kept things simple.

Her current cell phone had an ID block on it and Jeeves didn't have the number. So she told him she'd call him in the morning and rang off, turning toward the laptop instead.

Twenty minutes later, she craned her neck, listening for sounds from the guest room. Nothing.

She'd expected to find Ryder waiting for her when she got back from Gurtza's place. Surely he'd heard her return?

She clicked on a link in the browser, then scanned the Web site. There was an expanded piece on the estate fire in the local Wisconsin paper, but it said nothing about her beyond reporting that the owner was away at the time of the incident and couldn't be contacted.

The second part, at least, was true.

Seline shut the browser window and got up from the table, heading in the direction of the guest bedroom, her curiosity getting the better of her. Ryder was sprawled across the king-sized bed wearing little more than a towel around his hips. He'd obviously showered, but hadn't shaved, probably opting to stretch out for a minute on the bed first.

She hesitated in the doorway, her hand on the knob as if to close the door and allow him privacy. But a more primal part of herself, brought on by their trip westward and by what had transpired in the past hour or so, spurred her to step farther into the room instead.

I just want to see his face, she told herself. *Then I'll go and let him sleep.*

She drew even with the bed. His face was

turned in her direction and he was snoring quietly, a long shadow created by the morning sun slanting through the narrow window crossing his cheek. Her breath snagged in her chest. He looked so rugged yet so vulnerable. Like a mischievous boy at the end of a long night of being naughty.

Unable to stop herself, she moved closer until she could sit on the edge of the bed. It had been a long time since she'd watched a man sleep. She reached out and brushed a lock of his hair from his brow. So handsome.

Before she knew she was going to do so, she scooted until she lay next to him, facing him, wanting to just look at him. Trying to crack the exterior of the man she'd spent the past two days straight with. What kind of father would he make, she wondered? Would he be hands-off, choosing work over spending time with his kids? Or would he insist on being involved in every aspect of their lives?

She recalled Ryder mentioning his father and his parent's lament of not having any grandchildren to spoil. She smiled softly and cuddled a little closer to his long, lean body. She must have shifted the mattress enough to alert him to her presence, because without awakening, he rolled onto his back, the towel around his hips dropping off, and he absently reached for her and curved her body against his side.

Seline didn't need any more invitation than that.

13

RYDER had no idea how long he'd been asleep, but he was surprised when he awakened to Seline curled up next to him, her arm draped around his chest, her leg hooked over one of his.

He swallowed and allowed his eyes to adjust to the dim light from the open bedroom door. Was it night? It seemed the logical conclusion. But surely he hadn't slept all day?

When he'd emerged from the shower earlier, he'd gone in search of Seline, and had been mystified when he'd found her bedroom empty, her shower dry, and the Camaro absent from the driveway. He couldn't figure out where she had gone. Hadn't they driven two days straight to reach this house? What was so important for her to do that it couldn't wait until she'd had a shower and eaten something?

He'd intended only to rest a bit and listen for her return. Obviously things hadn't gone as planned and she'd not only come back while he was asleep, she'd climbed in next to him and dropped off to sleep herself.

He swept away a strand of her dark hair that clung to her chin and stared down into her beautiful face. Then he leaned in and did what he'd been longing to do since they'd left Wisconsin: he kissed her.

SELINE grew aware of a slight pressure against her mouth. A pleasurable, hot pressure. She lazily blinked open her eyes to find Ryder's intense face mere millimeters away from hers as he leaned in to kiss her again. She reached up and entangled her fingers in his hair and sighed up into him, welcoming the feel of his mouth on hers.

There was something decadent, primeval about being wakened from a dead sleep by a sexy man's kiss. And given the darkness and her sleep-clouded mind, she found it all too easy to give herself over to sheer desire. For the feel of his tongue against hers. His hard body pressing insistently into her softer one.

Ryder groaned lightly at her touch and the return of his kiss, gently spreading her thighs so he could position himself between them, resting his forearms on the bed on either side of her head. He brushed her hair back repeatedly, alternately kissing her deeply, then drawing away to gaze into her face in the soft light. Warmth suffused her inside and out. Desire. Need. And an intimate connection that somehow transcended both.

That reflection caused Seline's breath to catch in her throat. She'd thought she'd known romantic love before. She knew other forms of love, like that between a parent and a child. But this… What she was coming to feel for Ryder was oh so different. Frightening and exciting all at once. Overwhelming and empowering.

Common sense dictated that she not read too much into her passion-fogged thoughts. After all, she hadn't known him for that long. But another part observed that they'd shared more in a few days than many people did in a month or even six. Their time together definitely eclipsed whatever dates she'd managed to go out on in the past few years.

Besides, the risk taker in her demanded that she see whatever was happening between them through to the end. Not only see it through, but boldly welcome it and embrace it.

Ryder bent his head and kissed her again, lingeringly, tenderly. And she leisurely kissed him back, aware of the deep thrum of her heart, the languidness of her limbs. She felt that she could kiss him, just kiss him, like that for hours. The sign of affection was strangely as intoxicating and satisfying as physical release. He shifted between her thighs and she moaned. Okay, *almost* as satisfying.

It felt as if hot coals that had been burning inside her burst into flames at the not-so-innocent touch, threatening to consume her with red-hot need. She grasped his bare shoulders, reveling in the feel of his rock-hard muscles even as she widened her legs to allow him a closer meeting.

His erection pressed against the white cotton of her underwear, the sensation innocently erotic. When she'd chosen the panties, she'd done so thinking they wouldn't be having sex. Not tonight. Not after all that had happened and all that had yet to come.

Only this wasn't mere sex, was it? What Ryder seemed to be offering went far beyond that.

He cupped her breast through her T-shirt, squeezing her engorged nipple so that it tightened further. Then he leaned back and grabbed her shirt by the hem, stripping it over her head before bending to take that same nipple into his mouth.

Seline arched her back, encouraging his attentions and the ripples of sensation that went with them. He licked her breast yet she felt the movement of his tongue against the core of her, and grew increasingly aware of his erection pulsing against her swollen sex through the white cotton.

Restless to feel his flesh against hers, she reached for the elastic top of her panties, shifting to push them down then off the rest of the way with Ryder's help.

He seemed to pause above her, his silken hard-on resting against her slick opening.

Seline swallowed thickly. "Condoms…"

She didn't have any in the house. There had never been any cause to stock them since he was the first man she'd ever brought back here with her.

And she knew that he'd used the last of whatever supply he'd carried in his wallet.

She wanted to scream and cry simultaneously.

And it appeared he felt the same.

"I can withdraw," he said against her neck where he was kissing her.

Seline's hands rested at the small of his back, sliding over his hard rear then back up again, knowing that he was putting the ball fully in her court.

But she wanted both his balls in a place that didn't have anything to do with a sports arena.

She reached down and cupped his thick length in her palm. Amazing that such a minor part of the human anatomy could inspire such a tremendous reaction.

Her heart expanding in her chest, she positioned the head against her center, the flesh-to-flesh contact igniting a shiver along her skin.

He didn't move, so she did. Rocking her hips upward, she took an inch of him in, the small action robbing her of breath and saliva. He groaned and grasped her hips, as if prepared to immediately withdraw for fear of orgasm. She held still, watching him, then gasped when he sank into her to the hilt, filling her to overflowing.

Sweet Jesus…

The molten quality of the blood running through her veins seemed to make her heart work overtime in order to pump it through. She experienced an odd weightlessness in her womb that spread outward until it encompassed her entire body. He moved, slightly withdrawing, then thrusting deep again, heightening the unfamiliar feelings.

Seline realized she was trembling all over, and as she stared into Ryder's eyes she saw that he was fiercely trying to control himself and their unprotected union. His teeth were clenched, his jaw granite. Sweat beaded across his brow and his biceps bulged where he held himself rigidly above her, as if needing to watch her. To take in her every expression. To take her emotionally as well as physically.

Another deep stroke that coaxed a low, trembling moan from her throat. Then another. And before she knew what was happening, Seline threw herself head-first into the most phenomenal orgasm she'd ever experienced.

Or what would have been had Ryder not completely withdrawn and pressed his penis against her lower belly, his hot seed spilling over her quivering skin.

AN HOUR LATER Ryder sat across the open kitchen/dining area across a rough-hewn pine table from Seline, plates of food between them that they picked from with their fingers and with rolled fresh…what had she called them? *Sopaipillas*. She'd put out skinny glasses for tequila, but after knocking one back Ryder went for his water glass instead.

"So where did you go earlier?" he asked quietly.

Had he not been watching closely, he might not have noticed the slight hesitation in Seline's hand as she took a bite of guacamole-laden *sopaipilla*. But he had noticed. Not just that, but the slight blanching of her skin. Otherwise, she appeared unconcerned with his question.

"I had to go see someone."

"Anyone I know?"

The side of her mouth curved upward. "I don't think so."

"Male or female?"

Another hesitation. "Female."

She finished off her food, brushed her hands together, then refilled their water glasses from a pitcher.

The only light came from an overhead fixture that cast a warm orange glow over the table.

"Been a while since you've paid the phone bill?" he asked, stuffing another *sopaipilla* with refried beans, cheese and lettuce.

"No, I disconnected it from the box outside when I left."

At least she was honest. "Why?"

"Because I don't need you tipping off anyone so they can follow us here."

"I wasn't followed."

She ignored his statement. "Tell me, Ryder. What are you still doing here?"

Now there was a question. He slowed his chewing, thinking over how to answer her. Hell, he needed to answer the question for himself.

What *was* he still doing with her? Surely he should have left a long time ago. Probably back in Chicago when she'd pointed toward the hotels in the opposite direction to that she'd been walking. But he hadn't. And he still didn't want to leave.

"I don't know," he said finally, holding her gaze.

She nodded. "I suppose that's fair considering that I don't know why I haven't forced you to leave."

He grinned and sat back. "And how would you go about doing that, exactly?"

She propped her chin in her hand. "Not the whole me-Tarzan-you-Jane bit?"

"No. I wouldn't do that. After all, it was you who saved my bacon in Wisconsin." Ryder shrugged. "Never mind that you're the one who slapped it into the frying pan to begin with." He sipped his water. "You didn't answer my question."

"How I could force you to leave? Simple. I could have asked the guard at the gate to remove you from my car."

He was amused. "Here I thought you were going to outline the weapons you have stashed all over the house."

"Then there's that."

"You didn't have anything on you when you crawled into bed with me earlier."

She slowly shook her head. He got the distinct impression that she wasn't only thinking about literal weapons, but those of the emotional variety.

He could relate. He felt…strange, somehow. Altered by the sex they'd had tonight. Her musky sweet scent combined with his filled his senses and he was still semi-hard. Which was coming to be a regular state for him when in her presence.

"So what happens from here?" he said.

Her eyes darkened as she considered him. "Now you go home."

He grimaced, deciding it best not to say that option wasn't anywhere near the table, much less on it. "And you?"

"I…well, I put together the con of my lifetime. Not for money or revenge, but to save my life."

The wall phone gave a shrill chirp. Both of them stared at it, jarred out of the moment of levity her words had inspired.

Seline got up and answered just as Ryder heard the loud crack of something that could have been a firecracker in the distance…or a gunshot.

"Hello?"

A moment later, Seline dropped the phone and ran toward her bedroom. "They've found us."

14

SELINE'S adrenaline shot to new levels as she quickly dressed in jeans and a black T-shirt in her bedroom, then pulled out the armoire and gave the upper right-hand corner a smack so that a compartment opened up to offer a selection of arms.

Ryder was buttoning up his jeans and wearing a similar black T-shirt as he joined her. She chose a 9mm Glock and drove an ammunition clip home, then slipped the firearm into a double holster she'd fastened across her shoulders. She then picked up a matching Glock and did the same on the opposite side.

"You may want to lay low for this one," she said. "I can't guarantee I can look after you this time."

What she didn't say was that it was because she had others to attend to as well as him. One special person in particular.

"Using a round-about route, head to the community center we passed on the way here. There's a safe room there."

"Safe room, my ass." He pulled a 9mm from the selection, then followed it with a sawed-off shotgun. He fastened an ammo belt snugly around his hips, and loaded it with shells. "I've never run from a fight in my life. And I'm not going to start now."

Seline paused for a heartbeat, looking into his handsomely determined face.

"In fact, maybe *you* should head for the community center."

That made her laugh unexpectedly as she closed the armoire, shoving it back against the wall. "Stay close on my heels."

She led the way out the back door, hitting the lockdown button once they were outside. The gate guard's words echoed in her ears.

"They were asking for Seline Sanborn. And then they unloaded on the shack like there was no tomorrow. I'm sorry, I couldn't stop them."

Little had the gunmen known that the guard shack was made of reinforced steel and bullet-proof glass so that if something like this happened, the guard could get the word out to the other seventeen armed guards on the perimeter and at similar stations within the compound. As well, an alarm would go out to the other thirty-two off-duty guards to report immediately.

Crouching to make as small a target as possible, Seline ran to the house next door, then to the next one, scanning the area as she went. Behind her she watched Ryder do the same.

It was said that once a marine, always a marine, and Seline had to agree in Ryder's case. All he needed was camouflage paint and clothes to make the image complete. He was deliberate and vigilant, his entire demeanor exuding a sense of confidence that made her feel safer somehow.

She started to move on to the next house when she felt two things simultaneously: Ryder jerking her closer to him and the spray of adobe as a bullet hit the wall where she'd been standing.

"Down!" he quietly ordered.

She hit the ground so hard she ended up with a mouth full of dirt. Before she could grab her gun from her holster, Ryder was aiming the sawed-off shotgun and firing, hitting his target twenty feet away with unerring accuracy.

The shooter went down and she was yanked up by Ryder who, just like that, took the lead, pulling her after him.

A part of her wanted to balk at the macho maneuvers. She was used to working alone, taking care of herself.

A bigger part of her was glad she had a partner with whom to share the reins. A competent partner who had just, how had he put it? Saved *her* bacon, putting them about even by her estimation.

She easily met him stride for stride, stopping when he stopped, moving when he moved, the synchronicity of their actions not lost on her, even if she did question her own abilities just now.

That's what happened when your emotions were attached to your job...

"We need to cross the street," she whispered.

"It's safe here," Ryder responded.

"Yes, but what we're running toward is that way."

RYDER HAD THOUGHT their main objective was to remove themselves from the compound posthaste. He'd believed they were running away from something—namely the gunmen who had skillfully invaded the community—rather than toward something.

But as Seline once again took the lead he realized he'd been wrong.

Most human mysteries, he'd discovered, either weren't worth the original attention, or once uncovered revealed an aspect of someone you'd thought you knew that you didn't want to see. Like the whiz-kid accountant who had worked for him for nearly ten years who hadn't really been a kid…but, as they all found out, had a sexual predilection for them. Or his first college girlfriend, a pretty young woman sworn to save herself for marriage, who'd gotten an STD because she'd slept with everyone in his class, it seemed, but him—including the prof.

Then there was the financial assistant who would sneak out during lunch, generating gossip that she was having an affair, when she'd really found a private spot to feed the pigeons that no one else knew about. Or the janitor who had locked himself into the office of one of the executives. He'd been suspected of casing the place for a future theft; it turned out he had been taking his lunch break in there so he could catch a sports event on cable.

But Seline…

Ryder got the definite impression that her mystery might fall solidly into both categories at once. She likely had secrets that would surprise him but probably shouldn't. And ones that might make him wish he'd gone back to his safe, stuffy life in New York the first time she'd ordered him to.

He noticed she was leading him in a circuitous route, and silently commended her on her tactical instincts. She'd have made a great marine. That is, he thought as he appreciated her curves in her dark attire, if those working with her could keep their minds on the task rather than on her backside.

Finally, they approached a house that was dark and appeared abandoned.

"This is it," she said, rounding the place then looking left and right before unlocking the back door.

Their shoes scuffed against the kitchen tile as she slipped through a hallway into a living room. Holding the shotgun upright and at the ready, Ryder scanned the other rooms they passed. It appeared no one was home.

Seline stopped and he covered her back as she moved a picture frame and entered a code into a keypad. A portion of the wall opened, revealing a six-by-five safe box. Inside were two shadows. One he identified as Gurtza. The other he couldn't make out.

"It's me," Seline said, dropping to her knees.

The other shadow launched itself into her

arms. A child, he realized. A little girl of no more than seven.

"Mommy, Mommy! I thought you'd never come. Are you here to save us?"

AN HOUR LATER, in the cramped confines of the old pickup truck Gurtza had been driving earlier in the day, Seline sat between her and Ryder, cradling her daughter in her arms. Rosalina had long since fallen asleep, as had Gurtza for that matter, leaving her with a silent Ryder for company. In fact, after hustling the seven-year-old and Gurtza into the truck, then telling Ryder to head south, she hadn't uttered a single word to him. Although the questioning gazes had been countless.

Ryder couldn't seem to keep his eyes off the sleeping little girl, who hadn't always been sleeping, but had instead bugged Ryder about who he was and where they were going and whether or not she could climb into his lap.

The answer to the last question had been no and had come from Seline herself, the tone of the one word drawing her companions' stares.

"So that's who you'd gone to see." Ryder finally broke the silence.

Seline nodded, brushing Lina's hair from her face.

Lina had her head on Seline's lap, her legs on Gurtza's, and while she looked uncomfortable as hell, she slept like a baby.

Ryder shook his head. "You know, there's got to come a time when you don't knock the air from my lungs."

She smiled and looked out at the dark southern New Mexican landscape as the truck hit a bump and rocked from side to side, the old struts groaning.

"How old is she?" he asked.

"Seven."

He looked at her. "Were you married at the time?"

Seline bit on her bottom lip then shook her head.

"But her father knows she exists."

A statement rather than a question. So she didn't answer.

"And your chosen career, as legally dangerous as it may be, isn't the reason you had her stashed away at the compound?"

"No."

"Anyone I know?"

How did she answer that? While she was certain that Ryder didn't know Mario Trainello personally, being a New Yorker, she was pretty sure he'd be familiar with the name.

A name she didn't intend to share just then.

"Am I driving to Mexico?"

"Yes. Gurtza and Lina will get on a bus just on the other side of the border."

"Another safe house?"

"In a manner of speaking, yes."

"You're not going with them?"

She shook her head again, her heart breaking at the thought of being away from her daughter for another extended amount of time.

She looked down at the sleeping face, tears welling up in her eyes.

There had been a few sweet months when it had just been her and the little girl she'd named after her maternal grandmother. The instant she'd known she was pregnant, Seline had headed up to British Columbia and rented a small place near the Strait of Georgia. Months had passed and she'd grown bigger, decorating the tiny nursery and waiting for the arrival of her baby. Just hers. No husband. No father. No boyfriend.

And when Rosalina was born…she'd felt as if the sun had finally broken out from behind the clouds that had always shadowed her life.

While she hadn't enjoyed anywhere near the financial resources she had now, she'd had enough to see her through the first year of Lina's life.

Then Trainello had discovered she'd had his

baby, and that peaceful time she'd had with her daughter had been shattered. She'd taken measures to make sure Lina would remain safe…always. Even if that meant that she couldn't play an ongoing role in her life.

"It must have been difficult for you all these years."

Seline's gaze cut to Ryder's face. They passed a gas station and the lights illuminated his features enough to see the sincerity in his eyes.

There had been several times over the past few days when she'd experienced moments of kismet with Ryder. When he'd looked at her and she'd truly felt she was being seen. Felt his understanding and empathy and experienced a connection as firmly as a caress.

But this was the first time she felt as if she'd had her breath stolen from her.

"The men back there…and in Wisconsin… they weren't after you, were they? They were after your daughter."

Seline shifted uncomfortably, the moment of affinity gone as she snapped back into protective-mother mode. Lina mumbled something in her sleep and then rolled over, Seline's help guaranteeing that she didn't hit her head on the dash or accidentally kick Gurtza.

"Her father?"

"Look, Ryder, I appreciate everything that you've done. But that's about all the questions I'm prepared to answer at this point."

A couple of miles disappeared under the truck before he said, "Why do I get the feeling that's the last question you're going to answer ever?"

Seline stared into his handsome face, her chest growing tight even as the impending sunrise brightened the horizon just beyond his arm to a deep purple.

Why, indeed?

15

RYDER SAT quietly in the passenger's side of the truck as Seline pulled into a parking lot that joined a small motel and a greasy spoon just west of Odessa, Texas. It was after noon and four hours had passed since they'd dropped Lina and Gurtza off at a bus stop in Ciudad Juarez just over the border into Mexico. As the little girl had waved at Seline, he'd watched as the woman who ranked right up there with some of the strongest people he knew seemed to fold in on herself, and he was filled with an incredible need to protect her. To use his considerable resources to shelter her and her daughter. Take care of them. Allow them to live their lives together.

And he had every intention of doing just that. With or without Seline's cooperation.

With or without any future involvement with Seline.

She shut off the truck engine and climbed out,

heading for the restaurant instead of the motel she'd parked in front of.

"Don't you think we should check in first?" he asked, closing the truck door.

She didn't answer.

They'd stashed their arms behind a cactus just north of the border, and then had picked them up coming back, the hardware now locked in a toolbox in the back of the truck bed.

Ryder shook his head and followed Seline, moments later sliding into a window booth across from her.

For the first time since early that morning, it seemed, she met his gaze head-on.

"This is where we part ways, Ryder."

He blinked at her. He'd had a feeling that this was coming, but, still, hearing the words was like taking a steel fist to the stomach.

He didn't quite know how to respond. He merely read the determination in her metal-gray eyes.

Finally, he reached out and took her hands in his. "I can help you, Seline. If you let me. I can call New York today, now, arrange to have you and Lina and Gurtza flown somewhere safe, guarded 24/7. I can see to it that the person trying to hurt you is stopped."

He drifted off. Not because he didn't have anything more to say, but because Seline was shaking her head. "No, Ryder, you can't. You have no idea what's going on here. Do you think money can really solve this? Money, I have."

She slid her hands from between his and a waitress took that as a cue to place two water glasses in front of them and ask if they wanted coffee.

As soon as she was gone, Seline continued. "You're an unknown quantity, Ryder. Ever since you entered my life, everything's been turned upside down. I can't let that happen anymore."

Was she blaming him for what had happened in New Mexico? Just as she blamed him for what had gone down in Wisconsin?

"I'm not even going to ask you who you called in Santa Fe. It doesn't matter." It seemed to take her extra effort to swallow. "If you want to help me, then leave. Go home. Go back to New York and forget I ever existed."

"I can't do that."

Her gaze sharpened. "I'm sorry, but I can't let you do otherwise. I can't continue to put myself…my daughter at risk for you."

"Damn it," he said, more forcefully than he'd intended. "I'm not to blame for what's going on.

The sooner you accept that, the sooner we can figure out what's really happening and stop it."

She abruptly got up, left a five-dollar bill on the table, then strode from the restaurant.

Ryder followed.

He shouldn't have been surprised when she knocked on one of the motel-room doors and it swung open to reveal Jeeves and two other people parked in front of computers. But he was. While she'd made a couple of brief phone calls from the road since this morning, something like this took orchestration. An effort he'd apparently missed.

"You look like hell," Jeeves said to her.

Seline ignored him. "Do you have the bag?"

He handed her a duffel and she handed it to Ryder who still stood in the door.

"What's this?" he asked, weighing the bag in his hand.

But Seline had already turned her attention to the people around her. A young woman had on a headset and was working a phone line. A young man was searching for something on the Internet that Seline examined over his shoulder.

And Jeeves stood staring at Ryder as though he was an uninvited encyclopedia salesman who had just been asked to leave.

He unzipped the duffel an inch to find wrapped stacks of one-hundred-dollar bills.

He jerked back as if physically pushed. "I don't want this," he said, tossing the bag to one of the two double beds.

Seline looked over her shoulder. "It's your money."

"I don't want it back."

Jeeves chuckled and Ryder glared at him.

The other man held up his hands. "Hey, don't look to use me as your punching bag, mate."

Ryder followed his gaze to where he had, indeed, curved his hands into fists as if itching to bury one into the smug houseman's handsome face.

Instead, he leaned against the open door frame and crossed his arms, planting himself.

A moment later the room went silent but for the tinny sound of a voice in the woman's earpiece and the beep of the other computer as it pulled up another document. All eyes turned toward him.

Seline stood straight and crossed her own arms, indulging his desire for a stare fest.

Finally, she grabbed his arm and pulled him outside, snatching up the duffel as if it was an afterthought. She slammed the door shut behind her then shoved the bag into his chest.

"Leave, Ryder. You're no longer welcome."

She dug into her pocket for the truck keys.

"Here. Take the truck. Drive to Abilene and catch the next plane out. Or have your personal jet come pick you up, I don't care. Just don't lead anyone else to me."

"I haven't led anyone to you."

"Who did you call from Santa Fe?"

Ryder gritted his back teeth together. "I didn't call anyone. You disconnected the line. Remember?"

She turned to go back into the room. He dropped the duffel and keys and grasped her arm.

"There's one way to figure out if what I'm saying is the truth."

She waited.

"You're right. I did make a call. From the neighbor's house."

Seline looked angry enough to hit him.

"I called Coleman's wife's cell. A number no one would be monitoring."

"You underestimate those on my tail."

"Then tell me who it is."

She didn't.

"Look, all you have to do is call your people in Santa Fe. Find out which house they went to first."

"What will that accomplish?"

"If they went to your house, well, then, my call isn't what brought them there. If they went to the neighbor's…"

"I don't need to call anyone. I already know you're to blame."

"Check it out."

"Go home, Ryder," she said.

The quiet tone of her voice stopped him in his tracks. The statement wasn't said in anger or reproach or accusation. Rather in that one moment she looked as crushed as he felt at the thought of leaving her to fend for herself.

"Please," he said, cupping the side of her face with his hand. "One phone call. Check it out."

She shook her head. "I'm sorry…."

Then she turned and disappeared inside the room and closed the door behind her.

RYDER didn't plan on going anywhere.

Checking into the motel room next to Seline's, he went about setting up a network of his own. He called a cell company in New York and arranged to have four new cell phones in the name of a subsidiary of his company delivered to four different people: the first to Coleman, the second to his secretary, the third to his father out in Brooklyn. And the fourth to the P.I. he'd used to find Seline.

A fifth cell phone he arranged to have delivered to him at the motel via a carrier two-and-a-half hours away in Abilene.

Once it arrived, he set about finding a way to convince Seline that he hadn't been followed. But without her assistance, his chances of doing that were nil.

He talked to everyone, assuring his father he was all right, and checking to make sure his company was still viable via Coleman, then giving him and his secretary a set of instructions that had nothing to do with the company and everything to do with Seline.

Finally, he called the P.I. and after receiving assurances that no one had coerced or beat any information out of her as to the whereabouts of Seline, he asked her to check a little further into her background. Namely, to unearth who else wanted to find her…and who the father of her child was.

The sun was visible through the west-facing window when the answering call came in.

He picked up the cell. "Blackwell."

"Just the man I'm looking for," Kylie said.

"You got the information."

"I got the information and then some."

"Tell me."

"Are you sitting down?"

He told her that he was.

"Carol Lambert aka Seline Sanborn's real name is Annette Agostini."

She paused and Ryder waited, running the name around his head.

Then it dawned on him. "Of the New York Agostinis? Part of the Venuto crime family?"

"That would be it."

He hadn't been sitting, but he did so now, collapsing to the edge of the bed as if his weight had quadrupled.

The Venuto family was one of the most powerful Mafia families in New York City. Not a day went by without a mention of one of their members being arrested or turning state's evidence or floating in the East River after a pair of cement overshoes turned out to be incapable of keeping them at the bottom.

"Jesus…"

"You can say that again," Kylie said. "I nearly got myself killed when I asked a few questions at the wrong time and in the wrong place earlier tonight.

"Anyway, she's not solidly connected. Rather, her father is the younger cousin of the big don, given more to penny-ante cons than to any real involvement in the family business."

"Define *penny-ante*."

"A few thousand here and there, sometimes tens of thousands. One con brought in over a hundred thou, but that's the one he served a dime for so when he was paroled, he went back to the smaller jobs." Ryder heard paper rustling and imagined her turning the pages in her handheld notebook. "Annette, I mean Seline, has two older brothers, also in the biz, Sergio and Paul. The con biz, not the mob biz, although the older one was known to dabble in his younger days—until the big boss's second son felt threatened and ordered a hit that crippled the guy for life."

"Some family."

"You can say that again. Anyway, Seline was tempted to follow in her dad's footsteps after he was put away and when brother number two figured out that using a fresh-faced eleven-year-old could help him land some pretty good cash. He coached her on how to pretend she was lost in Central Park and appeal to well-heeled passersby, thereby gaining their trust and easy access to their handbags and wallets, and he took her to the track where she could convince gamblers that her father had left her behind. By thirteen she was pulling cons on her own, with a couple of juvie convictions for selling fake newspaper subscriptions and items from those school magazines that were never received."

Ryder had a hard time reconciling what he was hearing. While he was proud to possess his own share of street smarts, he'd never seen the streets Seline had grown up on. Or rather the dark alleys full of hulking shadows that could hide unimaginable dangers or provide protection if you knew how to use them.

The picture Kylie painted for him fit the woman he was coming to know. And made him feel that much more protective of her.

"So the people after her are the result of a con gone bad?"

"I wish it were that simple," Kylie said. "You said that she's got a seven-year-old daughter, right?"

"Yes."

"Well, I don't think I need to explain the birds and the bees to you, so just as Seline's the mother, you know there's got to be a father. And in this case, the father is Mario Trainello. Also known as the Train.

"Seline's daughter isn't just an average little girl, she's a Mafia princess to a father who can't have any other blood children after an unfortunate accident on the job. A child he very much wants to claim—completely."

RYDER couldn't be sure how long he'd sat in that same position on the edge of the bed staring at nothing and thinking about everything. But when he looked at the clock it was past six. He stepped to the closed curtains and parted them to find Jeeves walking by along with his two friends, apparently going to the diner for a dinner break.

Which meant that Seline was by herself in the other room.

As soon as the threesome was well inside the diner, Ryder left his room and made his way next door. He tried the handle to find it unlocked, then knocked briefly before opening it.

Seline sat on the edge of the bed, her knees pulled up to her chest as she talked on a cell phone. He noticed that she'd changed into a fresh pair of jeans and a tank top. She eyed him warily as she dropped her voice.

"I'm glad you're having fun, sweetie," she was saying, closing her eyes. "Give the phone back to Gurtza, okay? I love you."

There was something vulnerable in the intimate exchange between mother and daughter. Especially in light of the new information he'd unearthed. Ryder pondered whether his parents could have put him in the hands of someone else for his own wellbeing.

Or whether he himself was capable of such a selfless act.

After discussing monetary matters and where Gurtza planned to head next with Rosalina, Seline finally closed the phone. But rather than address Ryder, she laid her cheek against the pillow of her knees and closed her eyes, not saying anything at all.

SELINE was aware of Ryder walking across the room and sitting next to her even though neither of them had said anything. Despite her best attempts at objectivity, her pulse leapt at his nearness and she felt a bone-deep gratitude that he hadn't left. Although, lord knew that if he had treated her the way she had treated him…well, she would have hitched a ride to the closest town if that's what it took to get away.

"They're okay?" he asked.

She knew he was talking about Lina and Gurtza and she nodded with her head turned away from him, hot tears stinging the back of her closed eyelids. For the next few days Gurtza would move around, never staying in the same

place for more than twelve hours straight until
Seline told her differently. But her daughter was
well and even viewed the traveling as an adven-
ture of sorts. A vacation after spending the past
few years at the compound with few trips outside,
because to do so was a risk Seline hadn't been
willing to take.

Of course, she didn't kid herself that Lina's
hunger for travel would last long. Even a seven-
year-old would grow tired of moving around so
much and begin to long for an uninterrupted
period of time to replant her roots.

That's why it had been so important to her for
her little girl to have her time at the compound,
even if it meant that it couldn't be with her.

She felt Ryder's hand on the back of her neck
and to her surprise a thick sob escaped her throat.
She hadn't been aware of its existence and was
even more saddened at the evidence of weakness.
But when Ryder pulled her into his arms and
held her to his strong body, a maelstrom of
emotion ripped from her chest. She clutched him
almost desperately, helpless to stop herself from
baring her soul to the man holding her.

She'd lived for so long in an emotional
vacuum, separated from her daughter, from her
family, that she felt as insignificant as a butterfly

in the face of a hurricane. She craved connection beyond all else. Intimate, personal connection. With her daughter. With Ryder.

Of course, it didn't help that she'd done as he'd asked earlier and discovered that he'd been right. He hadn't been to blame for the attack on the Santa Fe compound. The armed men had made a beeline directly for her house, the neighbor's from where Ryder had made his one phone call all but untouched.

She clutched him more desperately. "None of this makes any sense." She laughed without humor. "Not to me, and I know all the details. You…"

He kissed her lingeringly on the forehead then the nose, using tissues he took from a box on the nearby nightstand to gently wipe away the dampness from her face.

"Me…I'm just waiting for you to let me all the way in so I can try to help you make sense of it." He curved his finger under her chin and lifted her mouth to his, kissing her softly. "They always say two heads are better than one."

And six heads were better than two.

Seline thought of Jeeves and Joan and Earl at the diner and forced herself to sit up lest she be discovered in a position of weakness.

"One of the biggest mysteries here is…why

are you sticking around?" she asked, squinting her tired eyes to stare at him. "I thought maybe stumbling across my location was a way to break up the monotony of your life. Rather than skydive, you jumped right into the mess of my life by way of excitement."

"Yes, but when I skydive, I usually have a back-up chute."

She smiled, then stopped. "Why then?"

He looked altogether too sober. And so damn handsome that she was determined to remember the expression on his face in that moment forever.

"Did it ever cross your mind that I might care about you? Care about what happens to you?" He shook his head. "No, don't ask me why. I couldn't tell you that beyond saying something stupid like, 'Why is the sky blue?'"

"Because of the way our atmosphere reflects sunlight."

"Smart ass."

She sat up straighter. "If what you say is true, and you're sticking around because you care about me…" She trailed off, uncertain where she was going with the statement. Oh, she knew Ryder was drawn to her. Just as surely as she knew she was connected to him in some sort of mysterious way that she couldn't begin to explain, either. They were fused together by need and extraordinary circumstances.

"Well, then, you must understand that there is no future beyond now," she said quietly.

16

HOURS LATER, back in his room, with Seline soundly asleep on top of the double bed behind him, the ratty bedspread leaving a crease on her smooth cheek, Ryder stood at the window going over what she had said to him earlier. Trying to make sense out of her words, and his gut-deep reaction to them.

Never had he felt so conflicted. So torn between what he'd spent his life convincing himself that he wanted…and what he wanted now.

Namely Seline. At any cost.

"Come on, Ryder," she'd said earlier, looking at him as if it was the most important thing in the world to make him understand what she was saying. "You're all about tradition and building a bridge to the future that'll last for generations of Blackwells. I'm…I'm a ghost. I'll never be a soccer mom or belong to the PTA or bake cookies for the school bake sale. If I entered a church, the place would probably spontaneously combust. I don't exist on paper. And I can never exist on paper if I hope to keep my daughter safe."

But she existed to him. More than any other person in his life.

"Can't you see?" she'd asked. "There can be no future for you and me. Can never be any *us*. There's you. There's me. Then there's Lina. And my first priority will always be to take care of my daughter."

He'd told her he knew why, though he hadn't needed to. And even though telling her what he'd uncovered might tempt her to slam the door shut on him all over again, question his loyalty and trustworthiness just for having sought out information on her, never mind finding it, being honest with her had been more important.

Besides, the details didn't matter. Not to him. While the situation was more dire than he could have ever imagined on his own, it was dire with or without names.

The knowing merely increased his desire to play the role of protector, not detract from it. With or without her cooperation.

Ryder rubbed his forehead. It was after 4:00 a.m. central time, which meant it was 5:00 a.m. eastern. Before too long, everyone would be up and back to arranging the con they'd begun carefully piecing together like a complicated puzzle. He'd gotten the feeling they were leaving him out of some details, but he was relieved to be included at all and didn't question them.

He heard rustling and guessed Seline was shifting in her sleep.

Moments later, her soft voice broke the silence, "I checked up on Santa Fe like you asked."

Ryder turned from the window. The way she was positioned, he wondered if she'd gotten any sleep at all, or whether she'd been working everything out in her mind just as he'd been doing.

"You're right. Your phone call wasn't the tip-off."

He experienced a relief so complete he suddenly felt exhausted.

"Come here," she said, scooting over on the bed then patting the spread next to her. "Lie with me for a while."

Ryder crossed, took off his boots, then climbed in beside her. She immediately curved her bottom against him and he draped his arm across her hip, pulling her closer still. The rattling of the old air conditioner filled the room along with cold air and he shuddered, breathing in the fresh scent of her hair even as he gritted his back teeth together.

Whatever it took, he intended to prove to

Seline that she did exist. Maybe not as Annette Agostini anymore. But as Seline Sanborn.

And if he had anything to say about it, perhaps one day as Seline Blackwell.

TWO DAYS LATER, the five of them were in Trenton, New Jersey, having taken a private jet that Ryder had chartered, and they were staying in a rundown rental house in a seedy part of town where the police were known to be scarce, and the mob even scarcer. Control central was in the upstairs master bedroom, with a wall of monitors and three computers tuned in to the cameras that had been placed in carefully chosen areas.

"Okay," Seline said after taking a deep breath then clapping her hands. "Let the games begin."

All the chess pieces were in place and the con that wasn't for money or an adrenaline rush but rather for the lives of Seline and her daughter, Lina, went into play.

Ryder stood off to the side, content to let everyone do their jobs. He leaned against the doorjamb, watching as the view on his father's button camera flickered to life, then he heard his voice. "Testing, one, two, testing."

"You're coming through loud and clear,

Number One," Jeeves said into a microphone. "Now, go ahead and buy a newspaper from the corner kiosk, keeping the front of the Trainello house in view as you do so. But don't wander too far away from the waiting taxi in case you need to give pursuit quickly."

"Roger that."

Ryder rubbed his chin, amused that his father had not only volunteered to take part in the con, but that he was doing so as if he'd been running them all his life.

"Number Two, are you live?"

"Depends on your definition of the word."

Seline smiled briefly. "You're fine, Earl. Just follow the script and you'll be done before you know it." She looked at a monitor that fed through a roof camera across the street from Trainello's Brooklyn brownstone.

"I'd feel better if I were wired."

"They'll check you before you get a foot in. And if they find anything, that'll definitely test your definition of the word *live*."

"Not funny."

"Take a deep breath, Earl. You'll be fine. By the way, have I told you how good you look in black?"

"That's comforting. Maybe my mother can

use the suit to bury me in, you know, if it's not filled with too many holes."

Ryder stood upright and walked further into the room where another camera was focused on…was that a Burger King wrapper?

"What are they doing?" he asked.

Jeeves looked into the monitor then pushed a button for a microphone. "Number Three, what's going on?"

The Burger King wrapper disappeared, giving a clear view of a car's dashboard and the street beyond again. "Me and the guys were hungry."

"You couldn't have waited twenty minutes?"

"The food will be gone in two."

Jeeves cut the voice feed. "Actors."

Seline had decided to go with four aspiring actors for the second act of the con and had supplied them with two Crown Vics—cars that Ryder didn't want to know how she'd obtained— and outfitted them in black suits with black ties and mirrored sunglasses.

They thought they were playing a practical joke on a friend of Seline's for his birthday.

If everything went down as planned, they wouldn't have to learn differently.

As Seline had said when they'd begun outlining their options in Texas, they were at a distinct disadvantage in that none of them could play a key role because they'd be identified off the bat. And while she didn't like using outsiders, she had no other choice.

"Is this a go yet?" Ryder heard Earl ask. "I'm starting to sweat. And I don't think real FBI agents have sweat glands. It's in the contract or something."

Seline looked at Ryder, then at Joan and Jeeves. "Anytime you're ready, Earl."

"That would be never."

"Go."

"Going. Over and out."

They heard a click, indicating he'd shut off his cell phone.

All of them stood stiffly in front of the two monitors that would show Earl's movements. He was spotted by the roof cam and stepped into Ryder's father's button cam the instant he pulled up to the curb in his own dark-blue Crown Vic. A pause, then he climbed out of the car, looking every bit the FBI agent. Well, aside from the way he stretched his neck before looking up at the brownstone. He mounted the steps and rang the bell. Ryder's father's button cam bounced slightly as he walked nearer the house to get a closer view.

The door opened. Earl exchanged words with the armed goon who looked up and down the street before patting him down then stepping aside to let him in.

Seline let out a long breath, accenting all their feelings. "Now we wait."

Until Earl reemerged there was little else they could do.

His duty, simply, was to act like an agent looking for a quick buck. A buck he hoped to earn by tipping Mario Trainello off that Seline aka Annette Agostini had turned state's evidence and was going to testify against him. And to notify Trainello that agents were on their way to the house now to arrest him.

Stage one of the con: With an imaginary noose hanging above his head, Mario would have to abandon his search for her, and instead look for ways to save his own hide.

"Shall I head for the taxi?" Ryder's father asked.

Ryder reached for the mike. "Yes."

"Not yet," Jeeves said, but Ryder had already cut the sound.

Ryder stared at the other man. "It'll take him at least five minutes to reach it. He doesn't move the way he used to."

"If he gets in too soon, he could tip our hand."

Seline looked between the two men. "Let the order stand."

"The Train's door is opening," Joan said.

And just like that, two goons hurried outside and down the stairs, very obviously armed, looking up and down the block before motioning behind them that the coast was clear. Then Mario himself emerged and hurried for the Mercedes that roared up just as he hit the curb.

Ryder looked at his father's button cam. He had just climbed into the back of the taxi. "Have him follow the Mercedes, Dad."

"I know."

Ryder smiled as his father played secret agent. Maybe everyone was born with a desire to push the boundaries at least once.

"Number Four, where are you?" Seline asked, referring to another car parked up the block and positioned to follow Trainello when he bolted.

"Right on his tail."

"Where's Earl?" Seline asked, reaching for the control for the roof cam.

"He hasn't come out yet."

"His car's still outside in plain sight."

Ryder watched as another goon came out and got into the Crown Vic.

"Shit."

Seline picked up her cell.

Ryder said, "Give it a minute. Maybe they're waiting to see if the agents show before they let him go."

Seline held his gaze for a long moment and then nodded. "I hate not being on the scene, not being in control."

He smiled at her and curved his fingers over her shoulder, feeling the steel-like strength beneath her T-shirt. "It's going to be fine."

"Should I tell the actors it's a go?" Joan asked.

Seline turned around. "Yes."

Ryder looked around the room, curiously finding one person suddenly missing. "Where's Jeeves?" he asked.

Seline's gaze darted about then she called out. No answer.

On the monitors two Crown Victorias pulled in front of Trainello's place at opposing angles. Doors opened and the four actors paid to look like FBI agents got out, drawing fake weapons and charging the brownstone.

But Ryder was more concerned about Jeeves' disappearance.

17

"HE'S GONE," Joan said.

Seline felt suddenly sick to her stomach. Jeeves had been with her for over two years, and she had only just come to completely trust him in the last few months. Relied on him, especially, over the past couple of days. Mostly because of what had been happening. But she also recognized that her growing need to trust Ryder had extended to others in her life as well. Including Jeeves.

His absence now told her how very wrong that instinct had been.

"Abandon base," she said, her voice cracking. "Now," she said with more conviction.

"But what about the monitors? The equipment?" Joan asked.

"Grab the radios, nothing more."

Ryder grasped her shoulders. "What's going on?"

She briefly shut her eyes. "All this time, I thought

you'd been the one to lead Mario to me in Wisconsin. Then in Santa Fe. Instead it was Jeeves."

"How can you be sure?"

"Where is he?"

Ryder's frown frightened her further.

They both watched on the monitors as the actors hired to play apprehending FBI agents knocked on Trainello's door, then went inside, coming out moments later empty-handed. Stage one accomplished.

Not that it mattered. The mission had been highly compromised. In fact, Seline now knew that she was a part of someone else's con. Jeeves'. And by extension, Mario's.

Ryder grabbed the mike and found the button for Number One. "Dad, abort the mission. Repeat, abort."

"What? I can't hear you—"

Static. Ryder watched the button camera go dark as the taxi his father was in entered the Brooklyn Tunnel.

"We need to move. The best I can figure is we have five minutes," Seline said breathlessly, helping Joan gather what they could into small duffel bags.

"It takes longer than that to get from Brooklyn to here."

"Trainello has people here. And if Jeeves is involved…"

"If Jeeves is involved, then they'll be waiting for us the minute we leave the house."

They hurried down the stairs to the first floor, but didn't open the front door.

Aside from the electric feed in the upstairs bedroom, the power had been cut, and the house was already dark since the sun had set. Seline couldn't tell shadow from person.

"What now?" Ryder asked.

Seline pushed the button to dial Earl's cell phone. She didn't like that they hadn't seen him come out of Mario's place even after the FBI actors had swept the place, supposedly for birthday boy Mario.

After she got dead air, a strange busy signal sounded.

"Damn. I think they have a cell jam on us."

"Are we in trouble?" Joan asked.

Seline and Ryder looked at the young woman as if just seeing her for the first time.

The sound of heavy footsteps came from the front porch, made by someone not even trying for quiet.

Seline found herself being yanked by Ryder into another room. There was a curtained window off to the side. He hurried her and Joan to it just as the front and the back doors of the house rattled ominously.

At the same time as the intruders crashed inside, Ryder broke the locked window, then lifted Seline over the sill until her booted feet hit a narrow sidewalk overgrown by weeds. He quickly followed after passing Joan through the window.

"They're going straight upstairs."

Which erased whatever doubt she may have had about Jeeves' innocence.

"No," she said when Ryder started toward the front. "We'll have a better chance going the back route."

"In the front we can hit the neighbor's porch and scramble out that way."

"Lead on."

He did and she wasn't surprised to find that he was right. The neighbor's porch was positioned in such a way that there wasn't a direct line of vision from the front of the rental house. He hoisted her up along with Joan, then followed, and all three crawled across to the other side and down and over the ground there until they came to the next porch. On house three, Ryder edged his way inside the open door, scaring a woman who was handing her husband a beer where he sat in his recliner. Two children under five sat in front of the television.

Ryder held his hands up, even though there was a gun in one of them. "There's no reason anyone has to get hurt. Is your car in your garage?"

"Yes," the wife said in a high-pitched voice.

"Where are the keys?"

The wife looked at the husband. He didn't move.

"Harry!" she shouted. "Give them the god-damn keys!"

"All right, all right. Stop your nagging."

Ryder took out a roll of bills and peeled off what had to amount to two thousand. "Look for more in your mailbox soon. Until then, tell the police you think two teenagers made off with your car. But wait an hour before you call."

The man accepted the money, then the woman snatched it from him. "How much more?"

"A lot."

Harry gave him the keys.

"You stay here," Ryder told Joan. "It'll be safer this way. Have some coffee in the kitchen with…" He looked at the wife.

"Margaret."

"With Margaret. Lay low until the sirens die down, then disappear for awhile." He handed her a fistful of money even though Seline had already paid her well for her services.

Joan nodded and hugged Seline. "Be careful."

"You, too."

Seline took the keys from Ryder and led the way to the door to the garage. The car was an old Ford that was more rust than metal, and when she started it up, the garage immediately filled with exhaust smoke from its lack of oil. Worse, they were probably heard at the house three doors up.

"They're going to spot us."

"Well, then," Ryder said, reaching across her to fasten her seatbelt buckle. "You're just going to have to lose them, aren't you?"

TWENTY MINUTES later they sat in a strip mall parking lot, Seline having lost the car that had given chase. Ryder sat quietly next to her, considering all that had happened. He had finally gotten through to his father via his cell, but it didn't sit well with him that the old man was now a known target because of Jeeves. He'd ordered him to have the taxi take him to Grand Central so he could catch a train for Boston, Detroit, D.C.— it didn't matter, just so long as he paid cash for the ticket and got out of the city now. Ryder couldn't be sure what Mario would do once he figured out Seline had slipped through the cracks again.

The one high point was that Earl had called Seline a couple of minutes ago. He'd managed to use a fire poker against the distracted goons at Mario's place and get out the back. He was told to do the same thing as Joan: disappear for a few days, longer if he could swing it.

Ryder looked over at Seline, who kept pushing Redial on her cell, her face unnaturally pale in the light given off by the streetlamps.

A strange busy signal sounded again.

"Let me try," he said, reaching out for her cell. She reluctantly gave it to him, but rather than try to use her phone, he entered the numbers into his, with the same result.

"Maybe Gurtza's somewhere where there's no service."

Even as he said the words, he knew they'd prove little comfort to a worried mother.

A mother who had told the wrong guy where her daughter was. Not the exact location—not even she knew exactly where Gurtza was traveling. She did, however, have a rough idea.

And so did Jeeves.

"So what do you think the plan was?" he asked, suspecting he knew the answer, but needing to fill the silence. He had too try to wrap his brain around what had gone down in the hopes of figuring our where they went from there.

"Find Lina. Kill me." She looked at him. "That's always been his plan."

"Drastic."

"Yeah, well, he knows if he leaves me alive I'll always try to get my daughter back."

Ryder stretched his arm across the seat and gently grasped her shoulder. The muscles beneath her T-shirt were tensed into steel balls.

"You know, we could always move forward with the con."

She jerked to look at him. "What are you talking about? There is no more con anymore."

He swallowed hard. "The next step was for Earl to tell Trainello the address of the safe house where you were being held."

"A safe house that was a set up to trap Mario." She sighed heavily. "But thanks to Jeeves, Trainello knows that there was no safe house because there was no turning state's evidence."

"You could always make it real."

She stared at him as if he'd just lost a few of his marbles.

And maybe he had. Maybe it was stupid for him to suggest that a woman who was used to operating on the darker side of the law turn to the law for help.

Or maybe it was the smartest idea he'd had.

"What did you plan to do once you had Trainello, anyway?"

"Get him to confess to certain deeds then turn the tape over to the authorities."

"A tape that would have been useless without a live witness to testify."

"The tape would have been his confession."

"The law's a sticky business. There's no guarantee that the charges would have stuck. Even if the authorities decided to bring charges."

"Then there's the media."

Ryder nodded. "I get that part. But news like that only stays news until the next scandal or natural disaster or a politician's misstep."

"Are you telling me I should really consider turning state's evidence?"

"I'm suggesting that it may be your only option now that your hand's been tipped."

Seline bit her bottom lip. Whether it was to keep herself from lighting into him, or to keep from crying, he couldn't be sure. But he gave her the room she needed to let her decide.

"There's another option…"

He squinted at her. "Go on."

"We could show up at the safe house and take care of the situation ourselves."

"Define *take care of*."

She looked at him.

She intended to kill Trainello.

He rubbed the back of his neck.

He couldn't blame her. He'd only lived a short time with the knowledge of Trainello's existence, and he wouldn't mind seeing him dead.

But wanting to see someone dead and actually playing a part in making that happen were two entirely different things.

"That would be akin to suicide, walking into something like that. We're two. Trainello's goons can easily number a dozen."

She didn't blink.

"What happens to Lina if something happens to you?"

"Gurtza will take care of her."

He wasn't surprised by her answer. He'd known from the start that she was the type to sacrifice everything for a cause. And for her daughter, she was willing to lay down her very life…and offer up his in the process.

She started the car back up.

"Where are you going?"

"To get us some better wheels."

That hadn't been the answer he'd been looking for.

But he did know that whatever Seline decided, he was in. Until the end.

18

THREE HOURS later, Seline was crouched down in the shadows outside an old abandoned warehouse. She'd often laughed at B movies that had included scenes set just like this. There was too much room, too many open spaces, too little safety.

But after having been trapped inside three houses in a row, she'd quickly come to appreciate the setting.

Rather than set things up at the fake safe house as had been planned, she and Ryder had decided to set things up here. They'd spent two hours booby-trapping the place, stashing back-up weapons, wiring up the equipment they had managed to salvage from the failed con.

Then, ten minutes ago she'd accepted the latest call from Jeeves, who'd been trying to contact her since shortly after they'd escaped from the Trenton property in the old Ford. And she listened to him explain that he'd heard a sound and when he went to investigate, he'd been taken hostage by Trainello's goons.

Ryder had motioned for her to play along, but she hadn't been able to. She'd told Jeeves he could screw off and to tell Trainello and his gang that they could meet her at the warehouse in half an hour.

Of course, she fully expected them to be there in a third of that time. And she was ready for them.

She caught a glimpse of Ryder closing his cell phone, his attention on a spot she couldn't see in the distance. Her heart lodged firmly in her throat. She'd gotten him to agree not to call in the FBI.

So who had he called? He'd already arranged everything with his father.

Shit, shit, shit.

She moved back into the shadows before he looked her way in case he suspected she'd seen him.

A long time ago she'd come to expect the unexpected. But certainly even she had had more than her fair share of surprises over the past week. She deserved a break, didn't she?

She squinted up into the cloudy sky. Then again, maybe this was God's way of making her pay for her crimes, no matter that the people she targeted hardly missed the money she'd taken. The mere act of taking something that didn't belong to her was a crime. Technically.

Just how high of a price was she going to be asked to pay?

Seline swallowed hard. Whatever it was, she'd pay it. No price was too high to guarantee the safety of her little girl.

A car pulled up into the cracked and weed-choked parking lot some hundred feet away. She grabbed her 9mm and switched off the safety.

Ryder's hand rested against her wrist, pushing her arm down.

"These are the good guys."

Good guys? There were no good guys.

Ryder motioned for the car to pull inside the warehouse and park off to the side behind a wall of empty loading pallets. And when all four doors opened and her two brothers, her father and a cousin got out, Seline's knees nearly buckled.

"Is that my little girl?" her father asked, pinning her with his steely gaze.

Seline met him halfway and stood looking at him.

"What's this I hear? You're in trouble and didn't think of asking us for help?" he asked.

She looked down, admitting that she hadn't considered calling her immediate family, if only because of the extended Mafia family to which they were connected.

A part of her had wanted to keep them safe by keeping them out of this. Another part wasn't afraid to put them in a position of choosing between her and their own lives.

Her father hugged her and she nearly lost it.

It had been three years since she'd last seen him and her brothers. She pulled away to look at the two other men in question. The last time she'd seen her older brother Sergio, he had been in a wheelchair and had been expected to remain in one for the rest of his life. Instead he stood in front of her on half crutches. She hugged him, then turned toward Paulie, embracing him and then her cousin Vinny right after.

"How… I mean, why…"

"I called them," Ryder said unnecessarily.

Somewhere in the back of her mind she knew that Ryder had to have been the one who contacted her family. She just couldn't figure out how he knew how to get hold of them. Or why he would.

"I thought we could use reinforcements."

Another three cars pulled into the parking area

in quick succession and Sergio motioned for them to follow his lead, parking inside the warehouse.

And just like that they weren't two, but eighteen.

"Reinforcements, my ass," Seline's father said. "Get out of the way or you two might get hurt."

IT HADN'T BEEN easy keeping Seline in the dark as to his plans. But Ryder knew that he couldn't have allowed the two of them to face Trainello and his men without more firepower.

He just hadn't figured how much firepower his spur-of-the-moment call to her father would scare up.

"You Ryder?" the elder Agostini said.

The man was a couple of inches shorter than he was, but easily made up that difference in girth, his build stocky and solid.

Seline had told him that her father had never really played a role in the family business. He'd chosen running cons over gambling and prostitution and protection rackets.

All Ryder knew was that he wouldn't want to run across Seline's father or either of her two brothers in a dark alley.

"That would be me," Ryder said, offering his hand. Angelo Agostini took it and squeezed to the point of pain. Pain that Ryder refused to show him. "Glad you could make it."

"Make it? You should have called me before now. Had I known what was happening, I could have stopped this a long time ago."

"This isn't any of your concern, Papa."

"The hell it isn't," he said, looking over to where Seline was strategizing with her brothers on where to place everyone. "You're my little girl. And that little girl of yours is my grand-daughter. I don't give a shit who her father is, both of you are my blood. And by trying to spill it, Mario might as well have shot at me."

Her younger brother cocked a brow at Seline. "And we all know how Dad feels about being shot at."

Ryder didn't know the details, but he got the hint.

And if he hadn't, the sawed-off shotgun the elder Agostini pulled out of the trunk of his car would have clued him in.

"How long we got?" he asked.

"Five minutes at most," Seline said.

"Well, then, enough of this lollygagging about. We've got a job to do."

And just like that, everyone scattered to take their places.

Ryder and Seline retreated to the back of the warehouse where they'd already mapped out a position behind an old safe that had been tipped over, and away from any doors a car could drive through and catch them unawares. They had clear sight of the parking lot and any approaching vehicles. And had at least three direct escape routes.

Not that he thought they'd be needing any of those.

"I can't believe you called my father," Seline said softly beside him.

He made out her beautiful profile in the dark. "I had to call somebody."

"Yes, but my father? Do you know what might happen?"

"I'm not sure, but I'm guessing that if Trainello doesn't give up the ghost, he's going to become one."

"Along with us, maybe."

Ryder nodded. "Along with us, maybe."

Her lingering kiss surprised him. She'd been in full combat mode since they'd relocated to Trenton and had begun implementing the failed con. The demonstration of affection rocked him back on his heels.

"Knock if off, you two," her father said from

the shadows somewhere behind them. "We can look into a ceremony after we wrap this up."

Ryder raised his brows. "Ceremony?" he whispered to Seline.

"Welcome to the family."

IN THAT one moment, Seline felt more confident than she had in hours that the situation might sway in her favor. She gave the roof of the warehouse and the sky beyond a brief glance and offered up thanks. She couldn't believe Ryder had called her family, but, boy, was she ever glad that he had. While she was concerned for their safety, their mere presence gave her back the strength that had been lanced out of her by Jeeves' betrayal.

The sound of a car—correction, the sound of many cars—then headlights cut through the dark warehouse as a line of vehicles made its way through the parking lot toward the warehouse. The lead car stopped just short, causing the others to stop behind it. And just as it had happened with her family minutes earlier, doors opened, bodies spilled out and weapons were cocked and aimed.

"Mario," Seline called out. "Why don't you come inside? It's long past time you and I had a talk."

All heads turned toward a car door that had remained closed. Then, finally, it opened and Mario climbed out.

It was the first time in six years that Seline had seen him up close and personal. All she could feel was contempt. And regret.

She felt Ryder's presence close to her side.

Mario walked with four of his armed goons inside the warehouse then stopped just inside.

"Where are the freakin' lights? I can't see a goddamn thing."

As planned, her brother triggered a single lightbulb that hung a few feet in front of Seline and Ryder, although they were still in shadow.

Mario shielded his eyes. "Where you at?"

Seline moved to step forward and Ryder grabbed her with his free hand. She looked at him for a long moment, then he removed it.

She stepped a few inches forward. Not enough to be directly in the light, but she was partially illuminated.

Mario grinned, making her skin crawl.

"Annette, baby. You haven't changed a bit. Still the hot piece you always were."

"Wish I could say the same of you," she said between clenched teeth.

The conversation that sounded more like two

people having a chance meeting on the street than deciding the life of their daughter made her pulse quicken further.

She noticed the cockiness in his swagger as he moved closer, stepping as much into the light as she was on her end.

"So…how's Rosalina? My daughter?" he asked.

He may have grinned, but his eyes shot shards of sharp glass.

"Safe. And away from you. Two things I intend to make sure are always the case."

He tsked. "Come on now, Annette. As her father, I'm entitled to see my daughter."

"Take your beef up with the courts."

He chuckled along with a couple of his goons. "Call me stupid, but I don't think the courts and me would see eye to eye on this matter."

No, the families of New York served as their own judge, jury and executioners. And she was high on Mario's wish list of those he wanted executed.

Seline's gaze went to another man who had stepped up out of the shadows to stand next to Mario.

Jeeves.

"What?" Mario asked, putting his arm around

Jeeves' shoulder and giving a pat. "You look surprised to see my cousin Gino from England." He chuckled. "Didn't know we had any family from that part of the woods, did you?"

"No, I didn't. Did you check his credentials?"

Mario looked at her then at Jeeves. "Didn't have to. His mother is one of my mother's long-lost cousins. Remembers when the family came over to visit when little Gino here was knee-high to a grasshopper."

"More like student to Hannibal Lector," she said. Jeeves chuckled.

"What I meant is, are you sure he's your cousin?"

Mario started to answer, then stopped, taking a long look at Jeeves instead.

"What are you looking at me for, mate?" Jeeves said with a grin. "The woman's trying to mind-fuck you."

"Am I?"

Seline knew the family and its interactions well. Given that they existed in a vacuum outside the law, trust was at a high premium. And the saying, "you're innocent until someone accuses you" was coined in her neighborhood a long time ago.

"What do you know?" Mario asked her.

She shrugged as if it was of no-never-mind

to her. "Enough to know that he worked for me for two years and I never completely trusted him. How long's he been working for you, Mario? For the family? Your father know how deeply you let him in?"

Mario threw back his head and laughed. "I think you're right, Gino. She is trying to mind-fuck me." His tone hardened as he took out a Glock and pointed it at her. "Just like she fucked me seven years ago when she disappeared with my daughter."

"If I remember my history, it was you who screwed me, Mario," Seline said, taking out her own firearm and pointing it at him. "Literally. By raping me."

19

RYDER'S adrenaline shot well beyond any water-marks from previous runs. Mario had raped Seline? Or was she trying to further undermine his position? Ryder couldn't be certain. What he was sure of was that he didn't like the thought of the pig having his paws anywhere near Seline, either invited or otherwise.

"Rape? You called what happened between us rape?" Mario asked, looking too cocky for Ryder's comfort. "I call what happened love."

Seline squeezed off a shot, grazing Mario's shoulder but otherwise leaving him unhurt. The warehouse filled with the sound of metal against metal as guns were cocked all around. Mario's guys aimed their guns first at Seline, then every-where else, trying to figure out how many people hid in the shadows with their guns trained on them.

If Ryder had had any doubts about Seline's accusation, he didn't now. She wasn't one for random violence.

Mario had raped her.

And Ryder wanted to kill him for it.

"Oh, come on, Annette. You know you wanted it. You were begging for it."

Ryder caught Seline's arm before she could squeeze off another round, this time aiming for more dangerous territory.

"Who's this?" Mario asked. "You new loverboy?"

Loverboy. Such an antiquated word and reference. Had someone told him that a man his own age had used it, he would have questioned their sanity. Even in this tense situation, he had to suppress a smirk.

"It doesn't matter who I am," Ryder said. "What does matter is what happens from here."

Mario looked around at his men. Then he smiled. "Look who thinks he's calling the shots."

Ryder wanted to let Seline shoot him.

"Is it true, Mario?"

An unfamiliar voice echoed through the warehouse. But while it was unfamiliar to Ryder, apparently it wasn't to everyone else present. Jeeves took a couple of quick steps back as if afraid he might be caught in the crossfire. And Mario himself looked suddenly nervous, even releasing the hand that clutched his grazed shoulder.

"Father?"

Ryder was aware of two people approaching the light at once. One came from behind him and was Seline's father. The other came from behind Mario, and he guessed it was no other than Don Giovanni Trainello himself, the head of the Venuto crime family.

Seline looked at Ryder. He resisted the urge to shrug but he was sure his own surprise was written there for her to read.

No, he hadn't arranged this. He'd merely called her father for backup. Angelo must have called Mario's father, hoping to defuse what had escalated into a very dangerous situation.

"Is what she said true, Mario?" Don Giovanni said, coming to stand next to his son. Even though he was a good five inches shorter, and thirty years older, the power he exuded couldn't have been stronger had he worn a sign announcing he was The Don.

"Of course not, Papa," Mario said, laughing nervously. "Who you gonna believe, your son or some two-bit slut?"

The Don smacked his son with an open palm, the sound reverberating off the aluminum walls.

"You kiss your mother with that mouth? You show some respect when you're talking about the mother of my granddaughter. A child through whom runs the blood of the Trainello family."

Ryder sensed Seline's growing tension before he noticed the way her hand tightened around her 9mm. For a second he'd believed that this might be all resolved with a brief conversation. Now, he was afraid that more power might be put behind Mario's efforts to take Seline's daughter.

He'd tried to protect her. Instead, he might have put her in deeper danger…along with Rosalina.

The Don crossed to stand in front of Seline. "Is she a good girl?"

"What do you think?" Seline's father asked, stepping up to stand next to her. "She's smart and she's beautiful. Just like her mother."

Giovanni nodded. "Please…accept my apologies on behalf of my ill-mannered son. And for any wrong he might have perpetrated against you and your family."

Seline didn't respond, so her father did. "Apology accepted, Don Giovanni."

The Don nodded again, then, after a long moment spent staring into Seline's face, he turned and walked back into the shadows.

Both sides still had their guns pointed at each other, and Ryder waited for someone to take the first shot. Or rather the second.

"Mario, go home. Now. And call your dogs off the mother of your child. No child should be raised without its mother."

"But, Papa—"

"Now."

Mario glared at Seline and her father, looking as if he might disobey his father's order. He finally turned and stalked from the warehouse back to his car where he waited for someone to open the door for him.

Within moments, Mario's goons had disappeared back to their own cars, the long line taking turns backing up so they could turn around.

And just like that, a violent situation was defused, leaving Ryder to wonder whether or not he'd just imagined the entire episode.

And pondering just where, exactly, he and Seline went from here....

IT TURNED OUT that they went nowhere. Because no sooner had everyone left than Seline herself had disappeared.

Two days later Ryder stood in his top-floor office staring out at Manhattan...and couldn't drum up the enthusiasm that it took to remove a paper clip from a sheaf of papers on the Stanton deal.

"Uh-oh," Coleman said from behind him. "I'm not sure I like that look."

Ryder glanced at his second in command over his shoulder. It had been over forty-eight hours since the party had broken up at the New Jersey warehouse, time he'd used to try to reinsert himself back into his regular life. The problem was, nothing quite seemed to fit anymore. Including Coleman's familiar observation.

"Edit that," Coleman said, sitting up and putting his own papers on the desk in front of him. "I don't think I know this expression."

Ryder sighed and turned from the window. "Forget facial expressions for a minute, John, and answer something for me."

"Shoot."

Ryder winced at his friend's choice of words. "How did you know Jenny was the one for you? I mean, the woman you wanted to marry and spend the rest of your life with?"

Coleman looked momentarily surprised by the question. Apparently he'd been expecting something of a business nature.

But it didn't take him long to sit back in his

chair, cross his ankle over his knee and grin. "Simple. I knew the moment I figured out I couldn't live without her."

Ryder nodded, put his papers next to Coleman's, then shoved his hands deep into his pockets.

He'd suspected as much. But in Coleman's case, he hadn't had to hire a P.I. to look for his woman. Twice. Hadn't had to wonder if she was safe, or whether or not he'd see her again.

He knew Seline too well to know that finding her again wouldn't be easy. She was the type who didn't make the same mistake twice. And even though the Trainello family—or rather, Mario "the Train" Trainello—was no longer looking for her or her daughter, he doubted that would make much of a difference to the protective mother. She'd disappeared from the face of the earth as effectively as if she'd caught a ride on the next space shuttle.

He rubbed the back of his neck.

"Coleman, I want to sign the company over to you."

John blinked several times. "Stanton?"

"No, Blackwell."

His friend looked as if he'd been jerked back by an unseen hand. "And why would you want to do that? You've spent your life building this company. It's in your blood. It's your legacy."

Ryder smiled slightly at the description. All that had applied and more…B.S. Before Seline. Now…

Now all he could think about was getting out from under his responsibilities to spend his time trying to find her.

And when he did…

He'd have to cross that bridge when he came to it.

He didn't kid himself that convincing her into any sort of long-term relationship would be easy.

But he couldn't do anything less.

"I'm not talking about giving you the company, Coleman. I'm suggesting that you step into my shoes as CEO." He fingered through the papers then laid his palm against them. "Hell, you practically run the company now as it is."

"Only in your absence."

"Even when I'm here."

Coleman looked down. "Yes, but without the pressure of official responsibility."

"Are you saying that makes a difference?"

John stared at him for a long moment. "Does this mean a pay increase?"

Ryder laughed. "It means a considerable pay increase."

Coleman got up and thrust his hand across the desk. "Then you've found your man."

20

As soon as the airplane reached cruising altitude and the seat belt sign rang off, Seline released the mechanism and then pulled her legs to her chest in the plush first-class seat. Outside her window, New York City was no more than a blurry outline quickly being left behind.

And she felt as if the thin tether to the heart she'd left there was being stretched to its breaking point.

Two days. That's how long it had been since she'd last seen Ryder's handsome face. Enjoyed his wide, one-dimple grin. Reveled in the feel of his large hands branding her soft flesh. It seemed a lifetime ago. And it would extend to be a lifetime because she could never, ever hope to see him again. To do so would only add salt to the raw wounds leaving him had rent.

But leave him she had. While Don Giovanni had called a cease-fire in her standoff with Mario, she didn't kid herself into believing it would last for long. No, she fully expected Mario would soon figure out he could gain a new ally by turning to his father for help in obtaining legal and physical custody of his granddaughter, the seven-year-old born with the curse of Trainello blood. Which meant that she would have to double up her efforts to protect Lina.

And the first way to do that was to cut all ties with everyone in her life, much as she had done years ago. Only now that list of people included Ryder Blackwell.

A small sound escaped her throat and Seline was surprised to find herself crying.

Never had someone outside her immediate family affected her in such a deeply personal way. In the days she and Ryder had spent together, she'd learned how to trust again. Had relied on him as surely as she relied on her own limbs. And had learned that despite the titanium wall she'd erected around her heart, she was capable of falling in love.

It hadn't been easy lying low the last couple of days while she'd methodically closed every one of her accounts, pooled her resources, then created fresh fake fronts so she could redistribute her monies into more secure accounts. It had taken her being in the city to do that. And being in the city meant that Ryder was never that far away from her. In thought or reality.

Just one last time, her heart had pleaded with her.

But there could be no more times. She'd played out her hand where Ryder was concerned. Aside from not wanting to further hurt herself, it wouldn't be fair to Ryder, either.

A flight attendant neared her chair and she turned to face the window, pretending to sleep even as her shoulders trembled from the tears she was incapable of keeping at bay.

"Miss, I'm sorry, but something's wrong with this gentleman's seat. Do you mind if he takes the free one next to you?"

She minded. But there was little she could do about it. She waved her hand without looking to indicate her approval then edged her sunglasses down over her damp eyes.

"May I offer you a tissue?"

Not the voice of the attendant.

A tissue was held out over her shoulder. Seline slowly took it, the familiar scent of lime filling her senses.

She jerked around to face the man in the seat next to her.

Ryder…

RYDER hadn't known if he'd made the right decision until he saw the tears streaking Seline's flawless cheeks and witnessed the unguarded warmth in her gray eyes when she saw him.

Oh, the decision to act on P.I. Kylie Capshaw's information was right for him. He hadn't known if it would be right for Seline. After all, she wouldn't have disappeared if she'd thought their being together was a good idea.

"You're going to have a rough ride ahead of you, son," his father had told him when Ryder stopped by to tell him what he had planned. "I never thought I'd meet someone more stubborn than you, more driven than you. Then I met Seline."

Of course, his father was correct. He and Seline weren't opposites, they were almost painfully alike. He suspected it would more times than not emerge as a challenging aspect of their relationship.

To his surprise, Seline launched herself into his arms. He quickly braced himself so that they wouldn't end up on the aisle floor, then wrapped his arms around her, holding her close and pressing her body to his.

This...this sensation of completion. That's what he'd been after. And, he guessed, it was what everyone sought without knowing that's what they were looking for. And it was something you could only find with one other person in your lifetime.

Now that Ryder had found his, he wasn't about to let it go.

"How…? Why…?" Seline pulled slightly back to gaze into his eyes. A fleeting smile flickered over her strikingly beautiful face. "Never mind."

"You didn't think I'd just stand back and let you walk out of my life, did you?"

She looked down and he realized that she had thought exactly that. Or maybe hoped for it.

But it wasn't what she had wanted. Ryder knew that as surely as he knew his own name.

Threading his fingers through the hair over her ears, he drew her closer, leisurely tasting the salt from her tears on her lips, drinking deeply from her hot, slick mouth.

After long moments that left them both more than a little hot and bothered, Seline cleared her throat, smiled at him, then sat back in her seat, grasping his hand tightly in hers on the armrest.

And they both stared out at a future that wouldn't be traditional, wouldn't be expected, but would be theirs.

Epilogue

Chulucanas, Peru, near the Ecuadorian border, three months later

RYDER stood on the sweeping terrace of an old Spanish villa shaded by palm trees, taking in the stunning panorama from the top of the highest hill in the Piura highlands. The South Pacific sparkled like a polished blue jewel to the west, lush, untouched greenery to the east. To the untrained eye, it would seem the large house was unprotected. And that's the way he wanted it. While the compound was guarded by an obscene amount of security, not one of the countless cameras could be seen as they blended into the natural surroundings.

"Check."

The girl's voice pulled his attention down a shallow bluff to another shaded terrace beneath the one where he stood. Off to the right Lina and his father played chess in a small garden alcove, the elder Blackwell scratching his head as he considered the eight-year-old's latest move. Gurtza looked up from a nearby loveseat where she sat cross-stitching.

"Actually, Miss Rosalina, I believe that's checkmate."

Ryder smiled. His father had finally gotten the grandchild he'd wanted to teach his favorite game to, and much sooner than he had expected. While Alan Blackwell had supposedly come down for a brief visit, he'd been there for over a month, and Ryder hoped he'd decide to stay longer. If the growing bond between him and Lina wasn't enough to keep him there, then Ryder suspected the longing gazes he caught him and Gurtza exchanging when they thought no one was looking might.

"Well, good evening, Mr. Black."

Ryder didn't move, his hands casually tucked into the pockets of his white linen pants, the hem of his matching shirt flapping in the light, balmy breeze. But his smile spread from the outside to the inside, igniting a warmth that had as much to do with love as sexual desire.

He slowly turned. Seline stood in the open balcony doors of the villa wearing a black bikini top and a red wrap around her hips. And, as it always did, his heart dipped low in his chest.

This was his bad girl. His passion. His heart and soul.

"Good evening, Mrs. Black."

If he found it amusing that he'd spend the better part of his life trying to prove that his name meant something, then had so easily cast it aside in order to help protect the women he loved, he wasn't saying. He preferred to focus on the here and now.

Seline was here. And apparently she wanted him now.

Seline crossed to him and curved her arms around her husband's neck, reaching up to rub her cheek against his then kiss him lingeringly. He pressed her closer and she closed her eyes, breathing in the scent of him, reveling in his nearness. She blinked open her eyes to see her wedding ring throwing off shafts of light from the sinking sun. While Ryder had spent a considerable chunk of change on the set, she'd have been just as happy with a plastic one out of a gumball machine. Either would be worth more than every payoff she'd ever reaped from her career as a con artist…put together. He thrilled her every night and every day, both in bed and out. And he was building a connection with her child while at the same time wanting to know when she might want another.

Together they'd created a safe haven for their new family and had found ceaseless passion in their bedroom.

A bedroom she had arranged for them to spend an entire, blissful night in alone.

Ryder kissed her so deeply he took her breath away.

"Shall we join the others?" he asked huskily.

"Actually, we're not expected until brunch tomorrow, Mr. Black." She opened the top buttons on his shirt then trailed her fingers inside. "That is if you'll do me the pleasure of being my date tonight."

His bright blue eyes sparkled at her, and his one cheek dimple came out to play. "I couldn't think of anything else I'd rather do, Mrs. Black."

He swept her up into his arms and she held tight, pressing her mouth against his hot neck. "Oh, and if we happen to have a little extra time, there's this…job I'd like to discuss with you."

Ryder carried her into the room and used his foot to close the balcony doors. "Trust me, Seline, there won't be any extra time…."

* * * * *

Wait! The wide ride's not over yet…
There's another bad girl on the way!

Don't miss: Stripped
by Julie Elizabeth Leto

Available next month,
wherever Mills & Boon® books are sold.

My Secret Life *by Lori Wilde*

*Society diva Katie Winfield first encounters
sexy bachelor Liam James, with his broad
chest and winning smile, at a masquerade
ball. Now Liam wants to uncover the
delectable Katie – from head to toe…*

Turn the page for a sneak preview…

*Available from Mills & Boon® Blaze®
in October 2008*

My Secret Life

by

Lori Wilde

Resentment pummeled Liam's stomach like a heavy-weight boxer finishing off his wobbly-kneed opponent. Reflexively, he curled his fist around the birth certificate autographed by his biological father. The desire to punch something was so strong he could taste it.

Raw, bitter, black.

For the last twelve years he'd worked toward this moment, worked and waited, and Delancy had pulled the rug right out from under him. What should he do now?

You'll go at him again. You picked the wrong time, the wrong place, that's all.

His mother had never wanted him to do this. She was happy now, married to a great guy and living on a farm in upstate New York. She thought he should just forget about Finn Delancy and be proud of everything he'd accomplished without his old man's help.

But it wasn't that simple for Liam. He couldn't let it go. Anger twisted him up inside. The place was filled with privileged blue bloods, no doubt many of whom thought they could treat people any way they wanted and get away with it.

Liam blazed a hard gaze around the room. Frivolous, pampered rich people throwing silly costume parties. If they really wanted to give to charity, just write a check and don't waste money on lavish celebrations.

You're richer than most of them.

Yes, but he'd gotten his money the hard way. He'd earned every penny of it, not had it handed to him on a platinum platter.

Adrenaline, anger and frustration coursed through him. He needed to dissipate these feelings. Needed to get a firm grip on his emotions. Exercise. He needed exercise. A run in the park never failed to give him back his sense of control.

He had to get the hell out of here.

But then something caught his eye that made Liam forget everything except the fact he hadn't had sex in almost a year.

There, on the other side of the ballroom, stood a gorgeous vixen in a French maid costume and she was staring straight at him, as if he were the man of her most forbidden midnight fantasies.

Coyly, she tossed her auburn wig.

Liam drove his hand through his own wig.

She licked her lips.

Drawing in a ragged breath, he hooked his thumbs through his belt loop.

Her eyes widened, and he saw a telltale red flush spread from her generous cleavage up her long slender throat.

His body hardened and he shifted, widening his stance, pointing his boots in her direction.

She lowered her eyelashes, dropped her hands. His gaze fell to the creamy inside of her wrist, and then tracked up her smooth, delicate skin to her shoulders. She peeked at him again and then slyly winked. Even with the barrier of her black mask cloaking most of her face, he was absolutely certain she was winking at him.

Boldly, Liam winked back.

Why the hell not? Sex was better than jogging for blowing off steam and after what had happened before with Delancy, he could certainly do with the distraction.

And she was one fine distraction with those shapely legs encased in lust-arousing black fishnet stockings. He could easily imagine himself tugging that silky material over the curve of her calf.

She angled him a long, lingering look.

He caught it, held it.

Quickly, she looked away again, but there was no mistaking her invitation.

Come play with me.

His blood revved hot.

She turned and walked away.

The thundering in his veins intensified. Curiosity grabbed him by the short hairs and hung on tight. Who was this mysterious woman? Did he know her? Something about her seemed vaguely familiar, but he couldn't put his finger on what it was.

She made her way through the crowd, hips rolling seductively, as aloof as the blue-blooded princess she undoubtedly was. When she got to the doorway, she paused. Her long fingers stroked the door casing as she tossed him a glance over her shoulder. She looked damned provocative, even in a room chock-full of people dressed in suggestive garb.

Follow me, her eyes whispered.

Normally, Liam wasn't the type of guy who allowed his libido to overrule his common sense. But he was horny and desperately needing something to salve his battered ego, and she was hot and willing.

Why not go for it?

You shouldn't let your anger at Delancy drive you to casual sex with a frisky member of the Ladies League simply to prove you can bed the social elite.

Maybe not, but his gaze was ensnared on her full, rich mouth that was clearly made for kissing. She pursed her lips, slowly blew him a kiss and then crooked her index finger.

This way.

Liam felt the impact of the gesture slam low in his groin. Simultaneously, hormones and endorphins lit up both his body and his brain. He gulped against the sheer force of the sensation. This French maid wanted to have some fun. Why shouldn't he be the one to accommodate her?

He shook his head. What kind of spell had she cast over him? His tongue was cemented to the roof of his mouth.

His eyes were transfixed by her lithe form. His nose twitched, suddenly sensitized to the scent of seduction in the air. His ears filled with a blinding white roaring noise.

She strutted off a second time.

Mesmerized, he watched her hips sway.

Liam went all Neanderthal then and lumbered after her. *Must have woman.*

By the time he reached where she'd been standing, she was already in the archway of another room. The place could have been completely empty. That's how unaware he was of the crowd jostling around them.

The French maid paused again, but this time she did not look back. Apparently, she'd assumed he would follow.

She was correct.

Sending her auburn curls bouncing over her shoulders with a toss of her head, she turned to the right and started down a long corridor.

Liam made a beeline after her.

People were all around him, talking, laughing, joking, drinking, but he could have been stranded on a deserted island or trapped in a timeless vortex. He was that focused on Miss French Maid's fanny as she slipped through the costumed throng.

She winnowed around a man the size of a boxcar dressed like Paul Bunyan and Liam couldn't see her anymore. He quickened his pace, but at the next doorway, Paul Bunyan turned, blocking his path.

"Excuse me." Liam stepped to his right.

Paul Bunyan moved in the same direction at the exact same moment.

Liam corrected, angling to the left.

So did Bunyan.

Was this on purpose? What was happening here? Liam frowned.

"Shall we dance?" Paul Bunyan chuckled, and Liam realized he'd been unnecessarily suspicious. By the time he got around the guy, he found himself faced with a long hallway filled with doors. His French maid had vanished.

"Dammit," he muttered.

It's all for the best. He was feeling much too vulnerable to be indulging in anonymous sex. That kind of solace, while great in the moment, wouldn't fix anything. It wouldn't make up for the aching for a real father that had dogged his bones since he was a kid.

He stood there in the corridor, staring at the doors, wondering if she was behind one, not wanting to leave in case she reappeared. A minute ticked past. And then another.

Face it. She's gone.

He turned to retrace his steps when suddenly the door behind him opened and a hand reached out to grab him by the scruff of his collar.

Long, manicured fingernails tickled the back of his neck and the next thing Liam knew, he was being hauled into a pitch black closet.

The French maid wrapped her arms around him and covered his face in kisses. At least he hoped it was the French maid.

She murmured something in French. He didn't understand the language, but he did get the gist of her suggestive message. He tried to take a step back to clear his head, but her fingers were frantically working the buttons of his puffy white pirate shirt.

"Slow down," he said, or rather tried to say. His throat was twisted so tight with need the sounds came out as scarcely more than an excited groan.

Her mind-boggling aroma, which smelled like a cross between apricots and stargazer lilies, filled his nose and shot up his desire. He could see absolutely nothing in the darkness, but the rest of his senses were fully attuned and ready to be indulged.

"What…how…who…" He wrenched out the words, unable to form a coherent thought.

"Shh." She placed an index finger over his lips. Her skin tasted forbidden.

He thought of truffles and Russian caviar and saffron, the most expensive spice in the world. His nerve endings blazed. In the back of his mind, far off in the distance, sounding as if it had been locked up in a dry, dusty trunk for centuries, his muffled conscience tried to get his attention.

Hey, sport, this seems awfully odd. Sexy babe coming on to you, no strings attached. You know there's always strings attached. Something's wrong. Pull your head out of the hormone soup. Think this through. Last thing you want is to be like your old man. Hey, hey…

His scruples got no further because his brain short-circuited, closing off everything except the exquisite glory of her hot little mouth on his.

MILLS & BOON

Blaze

On sale 3rd October 2008

STRIPPED
by Julie Elizabeth Leto

Last time Lillith St Lyon met sexy detective Mac Mancusi he fell under her spell. Now the delectable lawman is back and he wants to rekindle the magic! But could Lillith's dark secret prevent their passion?

FOR LUST OR MONEY
by Kate Hoffmann

Cameraman Zach Haas is gorgeous, adventurous…and ten years younger than actress Kelly Castelle! But vivacious Kelly has captivated Zach, and he's ready to prove he's so much *more* than just a toyboy!

MY SECRET LIFE
by Lori Wilde

Katie Winfield's secrets were safe until tempting tycoon Liam James came along. Now the handsome bachelor is insisting he wants to uncover the impulsive Katie…from head to toe!

SHADOW HAWK
by Jill Shalvis

Abby Wells, an agent for the alcohol, tobacco and firearms bureau, thought she knew danger – until she got herself kidnapped by gorgeous fellow agent Conner Hawk! Now Hawk is leading Abby into forbidden territories and *forbidden pleasures…*

Possessed by a passionate sheikh

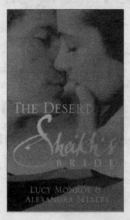

The Sheikh's Bartered Bride by **Lucy Monroe**

After a whirlwind courtship, Sheikh Hakim bin Omar al Kadar proposes marriage to shy Catherine Benning. After their wedding day, they travel to his desert kingdom, where Catherine discovers that Hakim has bought her!

Sheikh's Honour by **Alexandra Sellers**

Prince and heir Sheikh Jalal was claiming all that was his: land, title, throne…and a queen. Though temptress Clio Blake fought against the bandit prince's wooing like a tigress, Jalal would not be denied his woman!

Available 19th September 2008

Celebrate 100 years of pure reading pleasure with Mills & Boon®

To mark our centenary, each month we're publishing a special 100th Birthday Edition. These celebratory editions are packed with extra features and include a FREE bonus story.

Plus, you have the chance to enter a fabulous monthly prize draw. See 100th Birthday Edition books for details.

Now that's worth celebrating!

September 2008

Crazy about her Spanish Boss by Rebecca Winters
Includes FREE bonus story
Rafael's Convenient Proposal

November 2008

**The Rancher's Christmas Baby
by Cathy Gillen Thacker**
Includes FREE bonus story *Baby's First Christmas*

December 2008

One Magical Christmas by Carol Marinelli
Includes FREE bonus story *Emergency at Bayside*

Look for Mills & Boon® 100th Birthday Editions at your favourite bookseller or visit
www.millsandboon.co.uk